"COME ON OUT!
YOU'RE UNDER ARREST!"

Longarm tried the door handle and found it locked. He stepped back and shot the handle off, then kicked in the door and jumped back sideways, avoiding three gunshots. Everything in him wanted to jump back into the doorway and open fire, but he knew that was a good way to die, so he waited.

"You're under arrest for murder!"

"He didn't kill him!"

Longarm recognized the voice. "He's still under arrest for just trying to shoot me! Now are you coming out standing up . . . or down and dead?"

DON'T MISS THESE
ALL-ACTION WESTERN SERIES
FROM THE BERKLEY PUBLISHING GROUP

THE GUNSMITH by J. R. Roberts
Clint Adams was a legend among lawmen, outlaws, and ladies. They called him . . . the Gunsmith.

LONGARM by Tabor Evans
The popular long-running series about U.S. Deputy Marshal Long—his life, his loves, his fight for justice.

SLOCUM by Jake Logan
Today's longest-running action Western. John Slocum rides a deadly trail of hot blood and cold steel.

BUSHWHACKERS by B. J. Lanagan
An action-packed series by the creators of Longarm! The rousing adventures of the most brutal gang of cutthroats ever assembled—Quantrill's Raiders.

TABOR EVANS

AND THE WRONGED WOMAN

JOVE BOOKS, NEW YORK

LONGARM AND THE WRONGED WOMAN

A Jove Book / published by arrangement with
the author

PRINTING HISTORY
Jove edition / August 1999

The Penguin Putnam Inc. World Wide Web site address is
http://www.penguinputnam.com

ISBN: 0-515-12556-3

A JOVE BOOK®
Jove Books are published by The Berkley Publishing Group,
a division of Penguin Putnam Inc.,
375 Hudson Street, New York, New York 10014.
JOVE and the "J" design
are trademarks belonging to Penguin Putnam Inc.

PRINTED IN THE UNITED STATES OF AMERICA

10 9 8 7 6 5 4 3 2 1

To Dottie Q. in Lake Havasu

Chapter 1

It was a fine August morning in the booming Rocky Mountain town of Goldstrike, Colorado. U.S. Deputy Marshal Custis Long had just arrived to visit his old friend Town Marshal Wade Crockett, and enjoy a long-overdue vacation. His Denver boss, Chief Marshal Billy Vail, hadn't been any too happy about losing his best man for three weeks, but Longarm had not allowed himself to be talked out of yet another fishing vacation with Wade, his friend of over ten years.

At one time, he and Wade had each thought of becoming United States marshals, but then Wade had hiked up into the mountains to see if he could make a quick strike in the territory's newest boomtown. He hadn't, of course, but he'd met the daughter of a successful freighter, and had fallen head over heels in love. Three months later, Wade had married Rebecca, and when he'd gotten tired of looking at the back end of his father-in-law's contrary mules, he'd allowed himself to be talked into becoming the first lawman ever hired in Goldstrike.

Right away, there had been more than a few rough men who'd tested Wade's resolve and ability. But the newly hired lawman had bested them one by one, until he'd earned the respect of the settlement's rough-and-ready inhabitants and had tamed what had been one of the most lawless boomtowns in Colorado. Rebecca worried about her husband, and wished he had stayed in her father's freighting business, but since her husband had no interest in that line of work, she was determined to make him a good wife and to raise strong, God-fearing children; the more the better.

Over the years, Goldstrike had had its economic ups and downs, but the enormous size of the ore veins running east and west through the mountains seemed to indicate that they would last a long, long time. Furthermore, there was talk of building a railroad over the Rockies, and Goldstrike seemed to be a natural passageway across the great Continental Divide.

There was a lot of optimism in Goldstrike when Longarm arrived, and even better, the trout fishing in nearby Crystal Creek was said to be exceptional. Longarm was not a great fisherman, but he did enjoy taking a book and maybe a little sipping whiskey along and enjoying a leisurely afternoon. And if there happened to be a pretty lady who would also enjoy the pleasures of the day, then that made the outing even finer.

"I tell you, Custis, I wish that I made your money," Wade said as soon as his old friend arrived. "If I did, I'd buy me the biggest house in Goldstrike and retire."

Longarm knew his friend was teasing him, and replied, "Wade, if I had a wife as pretty as yours, I'd probably die of happiness before I got old enough to retire. How is Rebecca?"

"Can't wait to see you," Wade said. "She's been cooking up a storm, and tonight we're having roast beef,

2

mashed potatoes, and apple pie swimming in cinnamon and thick cream."

Longarm smacked his lips and uncinched his weary bay gelding. Dragging off the saddle, he pitched it over a stall divider in the barn behind Wade's house. "Last time I came to visit, I put on about twenty pounds," Longarm said. "And that was in just one week! Couldn't hardly get my belt to buckle the morning I headed back to Denver!"

Wade chuckled and patted his own round belly. "Yeah," he agreed, "Rebecca is some cook. If I didn't walk the streets constantly, I'd probably be fat as a hog. But you could stand to put on some beef. I'd say you were about twenty pounds on the light side."

"I've been working hard," Longarm admitted. "They don't give me much time to rest. Fact is, I had to practically wrestle Billy Vail in order to get this time off."

"Billy ought to be ashamed of himself for not wanting to give you time off now and then," Wade said. "I'll bet he goes through lawmen pretty fast."

"He does. I'm by far his senior man."

"I don't know how you put up with Denver anymore. Last time I was there, it was getting so crowded that a man had to look at a damned street map in order to find his way around! Why, here we all know each other. Everyone says hello and smiles. But in them big towns like Denver and Santa Fe, you don't know who is a friend or who is an enemy that maybe has it in for you because you arrested or shot his next of kin."

"I'm not arguing with that," Longarm replied. "But I believe I'd get a little bored in a town this small."

Wade scowled. "Bored? Why, Custis, there is always something exciting happening in Goldstrike! Just two weeks ago we had a shootout where a couple of fellas from the other side of the mountains figured they could come over here and rob not one, but *both* of our banks. And they nearly got away with it because they knew that I'd taken the afternoon off to go fishing!''

''So what happened?''

''Well, I heard the gunfire 'cause it ricocheted up the canyon. It started just after I'd hooked into what had to be the great-granddaddy fish of the whole darned creek! Anyway, I cut my line, dropped my pole, jumped on my horse, and came charging back to town to run into them just as they were leaving. We threw some lead at each other and I got real lucky.''

''You killed them both?''

''Naw, just one,'' Wade modestly admitted. ''The other is in bad shape, though. If he lives, he'll probably hang, so I don't think that he's getting the best of medical attention. We aren't big enough to have a real doctor yet, so that business goes to the undertaker.''

Longarm had to grin. ''It would seem like the undertaker might have his own financial interests in mind and want the wounded to die.''

''That is probably true,'' Wade confessed. ''But he's a good enough fella and wouldn't think of hastening the death of a solid citizen. Now an outlaw, well, that is another matter.''

''Let's go see Rebecca,'' Longarm said, untying his saddlebags and yanking his Winchester carbine out of his saddle boot. ''Is she still as pretty as before?''

''Gets bigger and prettier every day,'' Wade told him. ''We're expecting our first child next month.''

''Well, congratulations!'' Longarm shouted, pounding his friend's back so hard that Wade was knocked a few steps forward. ''Do you want a boy or a girl?''

''If it's a girl, I'd hope it was as pretty as Rebecca.

4

If a boy, as handsome as you, Custis. Are all the Denver women still fighting over you?''

"Naw,'' Longarm said, feeling his cheeks warm with embarrassment. "I don't even have a steady girl nowadays. I'm too busy hunting down outlaws to have time for romance.''

"That will be the day,'' Wade said dryly as they plodded up a dirt path that cut through tall weeds toward his modest little house.

Rebecca was every bit as attractive as Longarm remembered. She was heavy with child, and her skin glowed with good health and her lips parted in a big smile when she saw him.

"Custis, you finally made it!'' Rebecca cried, coming up and giving him a squeeze before stepping back and laughing. "Can you imagine this—I've gained all the weight and more that you've lost since you were last in Goldstrike.''

"I'm not exactly starving.''

"Not anymore, you're not!'' She linked her arm though his and practically dragged him up the back porch steps and into her kitchen. "You're going to eat like a king while you're staying with us.''

"I did the last time. I hope you like fish because I mean to catch a mess of 'em in the next few weeks.''

"We do,'' Rebecca said. "But they don't compare to beef, pork, or lamb chops.''

"I agree.''

Longarm was given the spare bedroom, which Rebecca had decorated in pink for their first child. "As you can see, I'm hoping for a girl,'' she said. "Sorry about all the pink lace and the bassinet and changing table.''

"That's all right,'' Custis replied with a wink.

5

"They'll be perfect for cleaning my fish and storing my tackle."

"Don't you even joke about that!" she cried with mock alarm. "No dead fish in my baby's room!"

Longarm threw up both hands in a gesture of surrender. "Yes, ma'am!"

Rebecca's face softened. "How have you been?"

"Just fine."

"You look thin and tired."

"I'm fine," he repeated. "And I'll put on more than enough weight while I'm visiting."

"I'll make sure of that," Rebecca vowed.

"Hey, Custis, come on in and let's celebrate!" Wade called.

Longarm squeezed Rebecca's arm and went into the small but neat and clean living room. Wade had already poured them each a glass of whiskey.

"My friend, sit down and take a load off your feet. How was your ride up into these mountains?"

"I had a good trip. Nothing eventful happened other than the usual sudden rainstorms."

"What about Cripple Creek and Silver City? Are they still booming?"

"They're doing well, but their mining stock has fallen, or so I've been told." Longarm pressed his hands against the small of his back, sore because he'd ridden too many miles in too short a time in order to enjoy this rare vacation. "I don't keep up much with that sort of thing."

"Where have you been lately?" Wade asked, lifting the glass and taking a deep swallow before smacking his lips.

"Billy sent me to Taos, New Mexico, last month to hunt down a killer and bring him back for trial. I was in Abilene before that, and down in Texas last winter after a gang of bank robbers. I caught up with them, but they chose to shoot it out rather than surrender. So it was an easy trip back home.''

Wade shook his head with amazement. ''You sure get around. Don't you ever tire of sleeping in strange hotels when you're in luck, and out on the trail when you're not?''

''Sure,'' Longarm admitted. ''But I still like the travel and the adventure. Nothing is worse than sitting around in an office trying to look busy.''

Wade's smile died, and his tone of voice was surprisingly sharp when he said, ''Hell, I don't do that!''

''I didn't mean that you ever did,'' Longarm said quickly, realizing he must have touched a raw nerve.

''Oh, I'll admit that I envy your exciting life,'' Wade added, trying to sound as if he hadn't been angry, ''but the rewards of having a family more than make up for it and that is the truth.''

''I'm sure it is.'' Longarm took a drink. He would have liked to have enjoyed a cigar, but knew that Rebecca didn't appreciate the rank smoke. ''And if I ever find a gal like Rebecca, I'll marry and settle down.''

Rebecca poked her head out of the kitchen. ''I have a few in mind for you, Custis! I've been telling some of my friends how handsome you are.''

''Great,'' Longarm said cryptically.

''Now, don't you go making judgments until you see these ladies!''

''No, ma'am,'' Longarm said, rolling his eyes at Wade, who had to cover his mouth to keep from laughing out loud. The last time Longarm had been fixed up with one of Rebecca's so-called respectable friends, he'd almost been raped and had had to fight his way back to

7

town. But he sure hadn't told Rebecca the truth.

"I've got a new friend named Eunice Oakley. She's a real peach, Custis. A little loud maybe, and perhaps on the heavy side, but she has the most beautiful smile and sense of humor."

"Sounds like a prize, Rebecca."

"Eunice is! And there is a new lady who arrived to open a millinery shop, and she is another possibility. I don't know her very well yet, but her name is Miss Gazella West. Now, isn't that a pretty name? So graceful-sounding . . . like a gazelle!"

Wade leaned forward to whisper, "Unfortunately, she ain't shaped like a gazelle. More like a hippopotamus, if you ask me."

"I heard that!"

"Sorry, dear."

Longarm relaxed and enjoyed the conversation. He noticed that Wade was drinking harder than normal, but attributed that to the strain of trying to keep the peace in Goldstrike as well as at home. Longarm had heard that all women could become a little testy during the final months of pregnancy, and he supposed that even included Rebecca Crockett, so he dismissed the trouble and listened to small talk until it was time to eat.

Dinner was as good as expected, and afterward they sat on the front porch sipping brandy while the sun went down and the stars appeared. Wade got a bit drunk, and when he nodded off for perhaps the fifth or sixth time, Rebecca shook him back to wakefulness. "Honey, you've had a long, long day. Why don't you go to bed now."

"All right," he mumbled. "Custis, you ready to pack it in for the night?"

"I'll be along soon."

"Night then," Wad

to be in the office all morn

the afternoon."

"Suits me fine."

"I ain't happy about having to work so

I'd expected to be able to take a lot of time o

you came, but things have a way of changing."

"I'll enjoy sleeping in," Longarm assured his friend.
"After I wake up, I'll drop by to visit you at the office."

"I'd like that. I got a new man I'd like you to meet.
Henry Tilson is his name and he's quite a find."

"Not so," Rebecca countered with pursed lips.

Wade frowned and looked at Rebecca, but she was
rocking in her chair and ignoring him, so he stumbled
inside muttering something under his breath.

"Rebecca, would you mind if I smoke?"

"Go ahead. It doesn't bother me as long as you are
downwind."

"I will be if I move my chair over on the other side
of you," Longarm decided, doing just that.

He lit a cigar and smoked in silence, occasionally sipping his brandy and glancing sideways at Rebecca, who
seemed lost in her own thoughts and the contemplation
of the starry universe.

"Sure is pretty out tonight," Longarm finally observed.

"Do you think he's all right?"

"Who?"

"Wade, of course. You must have noticed how much
he drank tonight."

"Not really. I drank about as much."

"No, you didn't. Not by half."

"Wade is just happy to see me and maybe get in some
fishing."

9

much?''

ave something

your friend and

,'' she blurted out,
upset about things all
nightmares sometimes

r to stay at the office nights
and Su   Henry Tilson one little bit, but
he was the   would take the job for the few
dollars the city   were willing to pay so that Wade
could have some time off. Tilson is not a nice man.''

"That isn't all bad for a jailer," Longarm replied,
trying make her feel better. "You don't want some soft-
hearted fella as a jailer, or the prisoners will gain his
sympathy and bad things can and will happen."

"Tilson is not to be trusted, but Wade seems to think
he is all right. They've gotten into some kind of side
business that Wade won't tell me about."

"Why?"

"My husband is obsessed about money. He says that
now that we are starting a family, he needs to save for
our children and our future. But they pay Wade only
enough of a salary to barely exist. We're always broke,
and it doesn't help that he is buying too much liquor."

Longarm didn't know what to say, so he said nothing.

"Tilson is also money hungry. He was a miner turned
gambler, and brags that he was once the marshal of a
town in Wyoming that he cleaned up fast. He will dem-
onstrate his ability with a six-gun at the drop of a hat.
Wade says he is very fast and accurate. I think Henry

Tilson is a deadly gunman who would like my husband's job.''

"Maybe he's just overly ambitious."

"He's smooth and charming on the outside, but inside . . . I have the feeling he is vicious at worst and a bad influence at best."

"Wade is a big boy and he's been around enough men to be able to separate the good from the bad."

"You'd sure think so, wouldn't you? But he has really misjudged Tilson. To make matters even worse, only yesterday I heard that the town council has decided to raise Tilson's wage from ten dollars a month to fifteen and give him a deputy's badge. Which means that now he can arrest and really intimidate people."

"And you're worried that he'll get your husband in trouble?"

"Of course!"

"Rebecca, what can I do?"

She reached out and touched his arm. "Just give me your honest impression of Tilson. If you think I'm being unreasonable, then tell me so right out. I trust your judgment."

"Maybe you should trust your husband's as well."

Rebecca's eyes filled with tears. "I probably should, but he's drinking far too much and not sleeping very well. All he has been talking about lately is money, and I'm sick of it!"

"I'll do what I can, Rebecca. You shouldn't be so upset right now with the baby coming."

"I can't tell you how much I appreciate your friendship. I've been counting the days until you arrived. I—I think I've even been more excited than Wade."

"Everything is going to work out fine."

"Don't say that until you've met Henry Tilson and

watched my husband. He's not doing well, and I can't talk to him about what it is that is so upsetting. Maybe you can, and then you can tell me.''

"I can't tell you what he confides in me," Longarm said, finishing his brandy. "Not unless it is vitally important that you know.''

"It will be!''

Rebecca climbed out of the rocker. "I'd better go in and make sure that he got to bed. Would you like some more brandy?''

"Yeah," Longarm said, feeling upset and wide awake now that he had this trouble to mull over. "I would enjoy that.''

"I'm sorry to lay this difficulty on you so soon. But . . .''

"Rebecca, it's all right. I'll get to the bottom of things and talk to Wade if necessary. But I can't push him too hard or too quick, because we both know how stubborn he can be.''

"Yes, we do.''

She lifted up on her toes and kissed Longarm, who was a good foot taller, and said, "Thank you for being our friend, Custis.''

"The thanks goes both ways. Good night.''

Longarm poured himself more brandy and smoked another cigar as he sat alone in the moonlight on his best friend's front porch. Down in the middle of town he could hear the sound of a piano and singing. A dog barked just up the street, and that set a lot more dogs to barking.

Soon, however, Deputy Marshal Custis Long didn't hear the piano music or the barking dogs. He was too lost in his own troubled reverie. Even if Rebecca hadn't confided her grave concerns to him he would have

12

known that something was very much amiss with Wade. His friend's laughter was too quick, forced, and strained. Furthermore, there was a haunted look in Wade Crockett's eyes that was shocking. *Rebecca is right,* Longarm decided, *something is very, very wrong.*

Chapter 2

Longarm slept quite late the following morning, and all the whiskey and brandy he'd consumed the night before had given him a raging thirst. Fortunately, there was a pitcher of cool water and a basin for washing, and he drank the water, shook himself into wakefulness, and dressed. He could hear Rebecca out in the kitchen humming a tune that he did not recognize.

"Mornin'," he said, coming to the table, where she poured him a cup of steaming black coffee.

"No sugar or cream, right?" she said.

"That's right."

She studied his face. "You look a little worse for wear this morning, but still much better than my husband."

"We'll live." Longarm slurped down the coffee, and Rebecca poured him another cup, then sat down.

"Custis, about last night. I'm sorry for—"

"It's all right," he interrupted.

"No, it's not. I—I get tired and upset in the evenings. I've had no energy and maybe things seem darker than they should."

"You're about to deliver your first child. I'd say that your feelings were normal."

15

"Perhaps, but when I'm upset, I get very worried. So I want to apologize for upsetting you last night. You were also tired and needed a good night's sleep."

"Which I got."

"I don't think so," Rebecca said. "You were upset about our conversation when I went to bed."

"Rebecca, I'm going to wake up, shave, and then go over to meet Henry Tilson and take his measure. After that, we can talk and I promise I'll be honest."

"Either way?"

"Yep. Good . . . or bad."

"That's all I ask. But what if you decide that Tilson is evil and leading Wade into trouble?"

Longarm stifled a yawn. "Did you ever hear the saying about how you can lead a horse to water but you can't make him drink?"

"Sure."

"Well, you can also lead a good man like Wade up to trouble but he won't bite."

"Even if he feels desperate for money?"

"That's right. There are a lot of desperate men, but they don't rob banks or turn to thievery because they are honest and know better."

"That's true, and Wade is as honest as the day is long."

"Of course he is." Longarm looked over at the stove and sniffed. "What's for breakfast?"

"Buttermilk pancakes, pork sausage, and more coffee."

"Sounds good! I'll start with the 'more coffee' part," he said, emptying his cup and making a mental note to stop by the general store and buy a whole bunch of food and provisions, as well as some cloth for Rebecca to make a dress or baby clothes.

16

It was almost eleven o'clock when Custis reached the jail and went inside. Wade was out, but a man who had to be Henry Tilson was sitting at the extra desk reading the newspaper.

"What can I do for you?" the man said, eyes flicking up from his paper.

Custis extended his hand and came forward. "I'm Wade's friend, United States Deputy Marshal Custis Long."

"Yep, Wade said you'd drop by," Tilson replied, not bothering to shake hands or introduce himself. "You can sit in his chair and wait. Shouldn't be too long."

Longarm's hand fell to his side and he slumped down in the chair. "Nice day."

"It's passable," Tilson said without looking up.

"You a fisherman?"

"Nope."

"I understand you've been a lawman in Wyoming."

"Yep."

Longarm was getting annoyed. "Why don't you put that damned paper down and look at me when I'm speaking, mister."

His tone of voice equaled the menace in his words, and Tilson slowly lowered the newspaper, then squinted across the room at Longarm. "Listen, friend, you can't come in here and give me your federal credentials and expect some kind of big welcome, 'cause I ain't impressed."

"I don't care about that, but I'm just not in the habit of talking to a newspaper. Where did you serve in Wyoming?"

"Up in the Wind River country near Lander. Town folded and so I came to Colorado."

"I see."

17

Tilson shook his head. "No, you don't, Mr. Federal Marshal. How much money you make a month?"

"I don't expect that is any of your business."

Tilson's eyes tightened around the corners and his lips formed a sneer. He was a big man, six feet and well over two hundred pounds, with a square jaw and prominent eyebrows. His nose had been fist-busted, and he had a ragged scar across his left cheek, which he tried to conceal with a three-day-old stubble of black beard.

"I don't guess we got a damned thing to talk about, Long."

"You might be mistaken about that. I heard that you are going to be given a badge."

"I have been."

"Congratulations," Longarm drawled without enthusiasm. "And what is this 'business venture' that you and Wade are starting?"

Tilson's eyes narrowed with suspicion. "Who told you that?"

"His wife."

"Rebecca is mistaken," Tilson replied. "Anyway, you want to know anything, ask her or Wade. I don't have time to chew the fat."

"Yeah, I can see that you're real busy."

That remark stung the man. He flushed with anger and stood up. "Mister, we just met and I already got a bellyful of you. Now either mind your own damn business, or get out of here and wait outside!"

Longarm stood up too and balled his fists. "I think we need to reach an understanding, Tilson."

"I agree," the man said, balling his own fists and hunching his shoulders. "All I've been hearing is Longarm this and Longarm that, and I'm sick and tired of hearing about you and all the great things you're supposed to have done everywhere you go. I ain't a damn bit impressed."

Longarm was ready to impress the man with the knuckles of his fists when Wade suddenly opened the door. "Custis, let's go . . ." His smile evaporated. "Say, what's going on here?"

"We were just about to get introduced proper," Longarm explained.

Wade looked at Tilson and flushed with anger. "Don't you know this is my best friend?"

"Well, he ain't gonna be mine," Tilson growled, scooping his hat off the rack and stomping past them and out the door. "I'll make the rounds, Wade. You and that sonofabitch can go fishin'!"

"Holy cow," Wade said, watching the man go. "What happened to set him off that way?"

"I think he's a little jealous. But no matter. Let's go fishing."

"Fine, but I need to go by the general store and get some fishhooks and line for your pole."

"Okay, let's go."

They walked along the boardwalk in silence until Longarm said, "Goldstrike is sure growing."

"You bet it is," Wade replied, glad to talk about something pleasant. "There's new folks arriving every day. We've got a school and two churches! Gonna start building a town hall next."

"How many saloons?"

"Eight, and two more due to open next month. You know how thirsty this high country can make a man. Maybe we ought to stop in for a couple of drinks and a bottle to take down to the creek and enjoy while we're fishing."

"I had enough last night to last a while longer."

Longarm followed Wade across the street to the town's largest general store. "Mr. Andrews still own this place?"

"Naw. He died and his widow sold out to a family called Iverson. They run the place now and no one is happy about it, but their prices and selection are still good. They're just not friendly. One of these days someone will come in with money and either buy or run them out of business."

"Marshal!"

Longarm and Wade turned around to see a large young woman with enormous breasts and long, muscular legs hurrying up the boardwalk. Her blue eyes were fixed on Longarm and she was grinning from ear to ear as she tried to smooth her long blond hair.

"Marshal Crockett, how dare you not come and introduce your tall, handsome friend to me!"

"Sorry, Miss West. Gazella, this here is Federal Deputy Marshal Custis Long."

Her eyelids fluttered and Gazella stuck out her ring-encrusted hand, palm down. Longarm sure hoped she didn't expect him to kiss the back of it, and so he grabbed her fingers and squeezed them hard.

"Pleasure, ma'am," he said, almost dizzy from her overpowering perfume.

The woman was undeniably attractive, in a lioness-like and predatory way. She boldly studied him from top to bottom, licking her lips with her moist tongue, and purred, "Rebecca warned me that you were a fine specimen of manhood, but I never imagined. Will you accept my invitation to come over tonight for dinner?"

"I . . ."

Wade cleared his throat. "I'm afraid that Custis and I are about to go fishing."

"Well, you can bring your smelly old fish to my house, but I was thinking of something a little more elegant. Maybe pork."

Longarm squirmed. Wade bit his tongue and looked away, shoulders shaking with concealed mirth.

"I'm afraid that I'm already engaged," Longarm stammered.

"To be married?"

"Ah . . . yes!"

"Oh, for gawd's sake!" Gazella cried. "Rebecca didn't tell me that! Is it real serious?"

"It is," Longarm told her, looking dead serious.

"Shit! Oops, excuse me!" Gazella covered her face and blushed. "I meant to say I'm glad you found someone. Is she pretty?"

"I think so." Longarm felt so sorry for Gazella that he threw her a compliment. "Almost as pretty as you are, Miss West."

Her eyes widened, and Longarm heard her sharp intake of breath. "Well, now, you sure are the sweet talker!"

Longarm tipped his hat and ducked into the general store because the woman looked ready to attack. Safely inside, he nodded to a sour-looking man behind the counter and started shopping for something to give Rebecca. "Morning! You Mr. Iverson?"

"I am."

"Well," Longarm said, "I'm looking for cloth."

"You'll find what we carry down that last aisle all the way back to the rear. Most of it costs ten cents a yard. Fancier stuff is marked higher."

"Thanks."

"Hey," Wade called, "the fishhooks and stuff we need is over here!"

"I know," Longarm replied, walking on down the narrow aisle to find the bolts of bright-colored cloth. His eyes were not accustomed to the dim interior of the large mercantile, and he nearly fell over the woman who was on her hands and knees trying to straighten out one of the low shelves.

"Miss, I'm sorry! I didn't see you down there."

"I should have said something to warn you." she replied. "It's so dark in here that it takes a while for your eyes to see well. I'm fine."

She stood up, and Longarm squinted a little to see that she was exceptionally beautiful. The young store clerk was in her early twenties, with shiny black hair and a voluptuous figure. She was also small, barely five feet tall. Longarm towered over the woman, feeling like an oaf in the presence of a pixie.

"Excuse me," she said, trying to squeeze past. "Mr. Iverson doesn't like me to waste time talking. He says I am being paid to work, not socialize."

"My name is Custis Long. I'm a good friend of the Crocketts. Rebecca—I mean, Mrs. Crockett—never said anything about you."

"I just arrived from the Utah Territory two days ago, so I don't know much of anybody yet."

"As pretty as you are, that will change quick. I'd like it to start with me."

"I'm . . . I'm sorry. I promised my uncle and cousin that I wouldn't take up with any customers, but would keep to myself and make no trouble."

"I'm not interested in trouble either. Who is your uncle?"

"Mr. Iverson. His son, Delbert, is my cousin. They're kind of rich, you know, and I don't want to lose this new job."

"I don't want you to either," Longarm assured her. "Could you show me what you have in the way of dress cloth?"

She brightened. "Why, sure! It's all right if I talk to you about merchandise. Leastways, I think it is."

Longarm followed her down the aisle to stop before a counter that had six or seven bolts of dress cloth. The light was so poor that he really couldn't see their exact color, so he said, "This is for Mrs. Crockett to make a dress for herself and her baby. What would you recommend?"

"Oh," the young woman answered, "they're all real pretty, but I like the one with the little pink roses."

"Sounds good."

"But it's fifteen cents a yard and you'll probably need five or six yards, Mr. Long."

"Please call me Custis. I don't mind paying that price. I'll take six yards."

"Yes, sir!"

"Custis," he repeated, "and you'd be Miss . . ."

"Dorothy Quigley. But everyone just calls me Dottie."

"Well, Dottie, how about dinner tonight?"

"You mean . . . us?" she asked, shrinking away.

"Sure."

"I can't do that! My uncle said that I couldn't do that or—"

"Dottie!"

Longarm saw her stiffen. "Dottie, I need your help up here in front," Iverson said.

Dottie started to jump forward, but Longarm caught her hand. "What's wrong with dinner?"

"Please, I can't afford to get sent back to Utah!"

Longarm heard the desperation in her voice and re-

23

leased the young woman, who then ran back up the aisle. He heard her say, "I was about to cut that tall fella some cloth for Mrs. Crockett to make into a dress. Honest!"

"I'll handle that," Iverson snapped. "You get a broom and sweep the front walk, and do a good job this time!"

"Yes, sir."

Longarm clenched his jaw as Wade came back and asked, "Is there something the matter with that new girl?"

"I'd say so."

"How much cloth do you want?" Iverson demanded the moment he joined them.

"You think Rebecca will like this?" Longarm asked Wade, ignoring the merchant.

"She sure will. But we're wasting fishing time. You can get that tomorrow. I got the hooks and line so let's get out of here."

Longarm reckoned that was a good idea, one that would give him an excuse to return tomorrow and try to get a little friendlier with the frightened girl from Utah. She was a lovely puzzle, and he couldn't imagine why she was so frightened about losing this job. Why, from what he could see, her uncle was a pure tyrant.

"Pa?"

They all turned as the back room door opened, flooding sunlight in from the storage and unloading area adjoining the alley. Longarm could not see the man's face, but he was tall and broad-shouldered.

"Pa, I got the wagon unloaded and everything stacked up. What should I do next?"

"Go up front and make sure Dottie isn't sloughing off with her sweeping," Iverson said.

"Okay!"

Longarm heard the eagerness in the young man's voice as he stomped up to the front.

"Well, you gonna buy dress cloth today or tomorrow or when?" Iverson demanded.

"Maybe never," Longarm said, taking a strong dislike to Iverson and his abrupt manners. "Wade, let's go fishing."

They left the mercantile, but not before Custis stopped at Dottie's side and whispered, "Sooner or later, you and me are going to have a nice dinner together."

"Shhh!" She was sweeping like crazy while her cousin glared at Longarm, muscular arms folded across his thick chest.

"I'll see you tomorrow," Longarm promised her as he and Wade headed up the street. Then he turned to Wade. "Why didn't you or Rebecca tell me about that young lady?"

"That's the first time I laid eyes on the woman, but she sure is a sight!"

"She's a looker," Longarm agreed, "and scared to death of her uncle and cousin."

"Yeah, he's stupid, but you wouldn't want to make him mad."

"I believe I already did," Longarm said with a smile as they headed back to the house to get their fishing poles.

"Hold on," Wade called outside the Rusty Bucket Saloon. "I want to get a little something to drink. Fishing makes a man thirsty."

Longarm followed his friend inside. Wade tossed down three whiskies, and would have kept drinking if Longarm hadn't grabbed him by the arm and dragged him outside saying, "Sun is high and we had better get to that trout stream before long."

"Don't rush me," Wade said, brushing off his hand. "I catch fish so fast it won't take very long."

"I didn't realize that was what we were supposed to do."

"What does that mean?"

"Nothing," Longarm said, trying to hide his disappointment. "I just thought we were going to have a long, relaxing day and swap a few lies."

"We will," Wade said, glancing back over his shoulder and starting to laugh.

"What's so funny?"

"Well, I just ain't sure, except that I was thinking we might invite Gazella over to join us for supper tonight, seeing as how you thought she was so pretty!"

Longarm banged his friend in the shoulder hard, and then they were both laughing.

Chapter 3

The fishing was everything that Longarm had hoped and expected. They were biting on worms, crickets, grasshoppers, and even some fancy ties that Longarm had bought in Denver, on sale because they were thought to be ineffective.

"You ever see anything to match this fishing stream?" Wade asked with a broad smile.

Longarm reeled in a three-pound beauty, but decided it was just too fine a fish to keep, so he turned it loose. "This is the best," he told his friend. "If I were a lawman like you and lived so close to this kind of fishing, I'm afraid I'd be derelict in my duties."

"Yeah, that is a temptation," Wade answered. "But with a child coming, I'm scratching and clawing, trying to find any and every way I can to produce more income. There's no future in being a small-town marshal. Right now I'm in good with the city council, but every time there is an election, I worry about how the political mix can change."

"That's a hard way to live."

"You bet it is," Wade said, "and I don't have to tell you that keeping my job depends far less on what I do than whose backside I have to kiss."

27

"After the way you came in and cleaned out the lawless element from Goldstrike, I can't imagine that they'd want anyone else to uphold the law."

"I don't know about that. Memories run short. I have to stay on good terms with all the right people, and their wives, relatives, and friends. Hell, I can't even kick a dog without first being sure who it belongs to!"

They both chuckled at Wade's humor, but then Longarm frowned and said, "Politics is less important working out of Denver."

"Aww, come on!"

"No," Longarm insisted, "I'm serious. There's politics aplenty with the federal government, but your fate doesn't usually depend on the whim of any local bureaucrats. I have a boss to please and that's about the extent of it."

"Is that a fact?"

"Yep. There's a specific and involved process that federal officials have to go through to fire a man, so that he has to have really screwed up bad."

"If I lose this job, maybe I should come down to Denver and you could help me get on with the feds."

"I'd be happy to introduce you to my boss with a strong recommendation. You could make quite a bit more money, but you'd have to travel."

"I know," Wade said, shaking his head. "And with Rebecca about to have our first child, that's no good. Also, I told you how I feel about big cities."

"That's a problem," Longarm agreed, tasting the sharp, clean sent of pines and admiring the picturesque surroundings. "I can sure understand how hard it would be on you and Rebecca to leave a town like Goldstrike."

"I love it here and will do most anything to stay, but it hasn't been easy. As you know, once I even tried to

28

work for Rebecca's father and become a mule skinner. They make better money than I do, but that wasn't for me. Her dad even put me in his office, but I was bored to death with all the invoicing and paperwork.''

"Paperwork drives me crazy too," Longarm commiserated. "I generally pay someone to do what can be passed along. For a few dollars out of my pocket, I save myself a lot of grief."

"Yeah, well, I don't have a few dollars. I couldn't pay someone pocket change, dammit!"

Wade hooked a small trout and angrily dragged it into his net. He tried to remove the hook, but it was set too deep and when the slippery fish almost got loose, he stomped it with the heel of his boot, cut his line, and tossed the dead fish into the stream growling, "That'll teach the bastard to fight me!"

Longarm was shocked by the shortness of Wade's fuse, but he didn't say anything. He was getting tired of fishing, and the afternoon sun felt so warm on his back that he was beginning to get sleepy. "What do you say we take a nap?"

"Naw," Wade replied. "I had better get on back to the office and see how Tilson is doing. I'll see you at the house about five o'clock."

"All right."

Longarm yawned, then removed his shirt and stretched out on the sandy beach they'd chosen as their fishing spot. He was not in the habit of taking naps, but he was worn down and it always took a few days to adjust to this higher altitude. A nice, sunny siesta would suit him just fine.

Longarm awoke feeling something warm pushing down on his chest. His eyes snapped open and his jaw dropped when he looked up at a completely naked Gazella unbuttoning his pants.

"Miss West, what are you doing!"

She giggled and shimmied her shoulders so that her huge breasts wagged from side to side. "I don't give up easily when I see something I really want, and I want *you*."

"Now wait a damned minute here!"

He tried to get up, but she tore his pants open and grabbed him by the balls.

"I think," she said sweetly, "you'd be a lot better off not to struggle."

"Are you thinking of . . . of raping me, or taking home a trophy?"

"Maybe both?" she said with a giggle.

If her reply hadn't been so ridiculous, Longarm would have put up a valiant fight, but he was still half asleep and this was—well, sort of interesting. He had never been partial to overweight women, but he'd heard they could be fun.

"Listen, Gazella," he protested. "I told you I was engaged to be married."

"Yeah, but you lied. I went to see Rebecca and she told me the truth, that you love to love lots of different women."

"So you decided to take matters into your own hands, huh?" he said nervously.

"I sure did! I saw Marshal Crockett returning to town with his fishing pole, and asked him where you was and he told me. So I just sort of—my, you're getting big!"

"Look, Gazella, this is a pretty well-traveled path along here and someone could come along at any minute."

"I live to take chances. Next to eating, what I like

best is to screw. So don't you dare disappoint me!''

Longarm knew that he should put up a good fight. Knew that he could even knock Gazella out colder than one of the fish in his creel, if he wanted. But the woman was already doing nice things to his manhood and, well, it had been a while since he'd had a good tumble; almost a week, in fact.

''Gazella, please let go of my balls or I might get real nervous and go limp.''

She released them, and then spread her muscular legs, whose thighs were much larger than his own. She had a round potbelly, and Longarm couldn't see what was actually happening, but when she slid down over his manhood, it sure felt hot and juicy.

''Ahhh,'' she sighed, wiggling down on him like a chicken on a nest of eggs, ''this is nice!''

Longarm laced his fingers behind his head and closed his eyes.

''How do you like me so far?'' she grunted.

''I like it just fine.''

''We're only just getting started, honey. By the time I'm finished, you'll be howling like a lobo wolf at the moon.''

He grinned. ''Gazella, talk is cheap.''

''I'm doing a lot more than talking,'' she panted as she moved up and down with the perfect, well-oiled precision of a piston rod.

''Yeah,'' he agreed, ''you sure are.''

''I'll bet you're thinking this beats fishing all to hell.''

''You must be reading my mind,'' he said, opening his eyes and looking up at those huge bouncing breasts.

Gazella rode him slow at first, like a horse that needed to be warmed up before it could be trotted or galloped. Pretty soon she must have decided that Longarm was warmed up fine, and began to move her hips faster.

"How are you doing?" she gasped. "You're not going to go pop-pop on me too fast are you?"

"I'll hang in for the whole ride," he promised.

"Good. Man, you sure got a big one!"

"I'm glad you approve."

She looked down through the cleavage in her breasts and blew him a frothy kiss. He could see that her cheeks were flushed and she was breathing hard. Her eyes were sort of glazed with pleasure and they were unfocused.

"Oh, honey, this is so good!"

Longarm reached up and squeezed her generous buttocks, which excited both him and her even more. Gazella began moaning and making funny sounds, and her huge breasts undulated like big ocean waves. Her lips formed a wide circle, and her tongue flicked in and out like a snake's. Longarm hoped that Gazella did not get too carried away and start bouncing, because that could be dangerous.

She finally climbed off. On her hands and knees now, Gazella brushed her long blond hair aside and looked back at him, saying, "Honey, I feel weak, I'm sweating like a pig and all out of breath, so it's your turn to do the humpin' for a while!"

Longarm peered down the trail toward Goldstrike, knowing that it was going to be tough explaining this if someone came along and caught them in the act. But the trail was empty, so he grabbed her wide hips and went at it with plenty of enthusiasm. Sure, he was tired, and the air was thin so that he was soon panting like a big dog, but this was fun, and Gazella must have been loving it too because she sure was making lots of noise.

After about ten minutes, he was exhausted and plenty happy to feel Gazella tighten up and then hear her cry out with ecstasy. A moment later, he emptied himself to the last, jerking drop of his seed, and rolled over onto his back, fighting for wind.

"Oh, honey," she whispered, rolling over next to his side. "We were really something, weren't we!"

"We were," he admitted. "I swear that I thought my heart was going to explode."

"Or your big balls!" She tittered.

"We've really pushed our luck," Longarm said, forcing himself to stand. "I think we'd better get dressed before we have company."

"I suppose," she replied, making no attempt to move.

"Gazella, you'd best be getting something on," he fretted. "I'm a stranger here, but you're not. If we were seen, it'd be a lot harder on you than me."

"Aw, most of the men know I'm easy. I haven't been in town long and my shop isn't doing that well, so . . . well, I've picked up a little humpin' money on the side."

"I never pay for it."

"Honey, I'd be plenty willing to pay *you*! When can we do this again?"

"I—I don't know."

Her lips formed a pout and she began to get dressed. "You sayin' this is it? That you can walk away from what I am willing to supply free and in great supply?"

"No," he replied, weakening. "That's not what I am saying."

"Well, then?"

"Look, Gazella. I like you and I sure liked the good times we just had, but the Crocketts are old-time friends and I don't want to embarrass them or myself."

Gazella angrily brushed back the tangles of her hair and used her dress to mop her face dry. "What about me?"

33

"Let's just . . . well, give it a day or two," Longarm said. "I'm pretty run-down and I need some rest. Humping has taken more energy than if I'd walked all the way up here from Denver!"

Her anger evaporated and she laughed loudly and obscenely. "I'm going to take that as a compliment."

"Good," he said, "and we'll do this again, I promise."

"Don't keep me waiting," she warned. "In case you haven't noticed, there are a lot more men than women up in these gold camps."

"I know," he told her. "And that's why I'm wondering why you chose me."

"Because of Rebecca and her husband. They were excited about your visit and told me all about you. She mentioned how you were tall and broad-shouldered and had to fight off the women. Well, that got me real interested, and I started having fantasies about you every night. And so, you could have been a bald midget when we met and I'd still have wanted you to give me a good screwin'."

Longarm chuckled. "You best get back to town now. I'll come along directly."

"You could come by later tonight," she said, pulling on her dress. "I live on First Street. Little yellow house with wild roses on the picket fence. But if the light on the porch is out, you might have to wait for a fella to leave first."

"I'll keep that in mind."

"I don't think you're going to come by," she said, her smile fading. "I just got a feeling that, once you have a gal like me, you're on the lookout for another."

"That's not true."

"Well, I sure hope not, because you are hung like a

stud horse and you've got stamina. I can only imagine what you could do to me if you was rested and we were humpin' at sea level or even down in Denver.''

"You're crazy," he said with a laugh.

"Yeah, well, I might come down to Denver just to get a good ride offa you if you don't come by at least once before you leave town."

"That sounds like a warning."

"It's a promise." Gazella kissed him, forcing her tongue into his mouth and grabbing his aching balls at the same time. She gave them a little squeeze and then retreated, slipping on her shoes and heading back down the trail.

"Some woman," Longarm said to himself. "She'd kill a much weaker man in a week or two for certain."

That evening after dinner, Longarm was still feeling the effects of his sexual extravagance, and his chin was bouncing off his chest when Wade finally left the porch and went inside to bed.

"Custis, you sure look exhausted," Rebecca said. "You'd best go in to bed right now."

He roused himself and started rocking in his chair. "I'll be fine, Rebecca. It's just the altitude."

"You must have hiked way up the stream, huh?"

"Yeah," he lied, "quite a ways."

"No need to do that," she told him. "I've heard that the fishing is pretty good just a little ways up the trail."

"Huh," he grunted. "Well, I won't go so far then."

"What did you think of Henry Tilson?"

"Rebecca, I only met him today and for just a few minutes before Wade came into the office and then dragged me out to go fishing."

"I'll bet he made you stop by a saloon first."

"We had a drink or two."

Her expression turned sad. "I don't want to get into Wade's drinking tonight. Just tell me what you thought of Tilson. Be real honest."

"I'd never lie to you."

"You might if you thought it would spare me worry or my feelings."

"I'd rather not say anything about Tilson right now, except that we didn't hit it off too well. He's not a very friendly man."

"He's dangerous, Curtis."

"Let me take a little longer before I come to a conclusion. All right?"

"All right," she agreed. "But I think you've already judged him as I have and you're wondering why Wade would allow a man like that in his office."

"I'm tired tonight," Longarm said, "and you need to get to sleep as well. I promise you we will talk about these things in great length over the next few days. I just don't think this is a good time."

"Why not?"

"Because we are tired and the hour is late. Things tend to always seem worse at night. Let's talk when we're rested and sitting here in the sunshine feeling happier."

"All right," she agreed. "But when you tell me that I'm right to be worried about my husband being around that man, you can then tell me what kind of business or arrangement they'd made together and how to end it."

"I will," Longarm promised. "I'll do whatever is necessary to see that Wade gets through whatever is wrong."

"Custis," she said, rising heavily from her own chair, "I do love Wade and I do love you too."

Longarm nodded, then went to bed, not trusting himself with words. He fell asleep thinking of Dottie in the general store, and of Gazella and all the fish he'd caught. All in all, it had been one hell of a fine day.

Chapter 4

Longarm arrived at Wade's office at nine o'clock the following morning with the idea of having a talk with him about Deputy Tilson. It wasn't something that he wanted to do, but Rebecca had again pleaded with him to investigate the new deputy, or at least try to delve into his past.

"If he's as rotten as I suspect and you can prove it to Wade, he'll have no choice but to force Tilson to resign," she'd reasoned.

But when Longarm arrived at the marshal's office, it was locked up tight. He frowned and decided that Wade and Tilson must have gone somewhere for a cup of coffee, or maybe even to answer a call for help.

Longarm stretched and yawned. He looked up and down the street and when Gazella appeared, he realized that he had better duck for cover before he was spotted. He chose to enter Iverson's mercantile in the hope of seeing Dottie and maybe taking her out for a late breakfast or asking her to lunch.

"Good morning," he said cheerfully to the stern-faced proprietor. "Fine day, isn't it."

"What's so good about it?" Iverson demanded. "You

39

come to buy some of that cloth or just to bother my niece?''

Longarm bristled, but when he saw Dottie standing just a ways down the aisle, he decided that she was worth taking some guff. ''I came to look at the cloth again.''

''It is exactly the same as it was yesterday.''

Longarm turned on his heel and went to visit with the girl. It was as dim in the place as usual, but he could see she looked pleased at his return.

''Good morning, Miss Quigley.''

''Good morning, sir. How are you today?''

''I'm fine. Just fine.''

''How was your fishing?''

''It was fine too,'' he replied.

''You look like you got a sunburn. You should wear your hat out in the sun. People think that just because we are in the high mountains they can't get a burn, but that is obviously not true.''

Longarm nodded with agreement, glad that she couldn't see his badly sunburned buttocks. ''I'd like to take you out for lunch,'' he said. ''What time do you eat?''

Dottie's sweet smile vanished. ''Oh, I couldn't do that with a customer!''

''Oh, yeah, I remember. You're not supposed to socialize with the customers.''

''That's right.'' Dottie gave a nervous glance up the aisle toward her boss. ''Would you like to see some yardage?''

''What?''

''Dress material.''

''Sure.''

Longarm listened without much interest as Dottie told

him prices and suggested how much he ought to buy. "If it was just a dress, I'd say that three yards would be enough. But if Rebecca wants to make some matching clothes for her new baby, she'll need at least five or six yards."

"Which do you like best?"

"Well, I like them all. But like I said yesterday, I especially admire this pale yellow one with the pink roses."

"That's the one I like best too," he told her. "Cut it for me."

"I'll do that, Dottie," a voice growled. "You go straighten up the shelves in the front."

Longarm and Dottie turned to face the young Iverson, who was glaring at them with disapproval.

"I'd prefer that the young lady cut the cloth, friend."

"My name ain't friend. It's Delbert Iverson. My pa owns this store and what we say goes."

"Get lost, because we don't need your help. Or better yet, go straighten those shelves yourself."

"No!" Dottie exclaimed, hand flying to her mouth. "I mean, I'll go up front. Delbert, you can do the cutting."

She started to hurry off, but Longarm stepped into her path, blocking the aisle. He turned his back on the big man and asked, "Why are you so frightened by these people? With your looks and personality, you could get a job almost anywhere in Goldstrike. For that matter, you could make a whole lot more money and have more fun working in Denver. That's where I'm from and—"

Longarm stiffened with pain when Delbert clamped an iron fist down on his left shoulder and pinched the nerve so hard it momentarily paralyzed his lower arm. Acting instinctively, he drove his right elbow backward in a vicious arc that caught Delbert in the solar plexus

41

and doubled him up. Longarm spun around, stomped the man's foot hard enough to break his toes, and then leveled him with a straight right cross to the side of his jaw.

Delbert crashed into the shelves, sending cans and bottles flying. His head slammed down on the wooden floor, bounced up and down, and then rolled to the side.

"Oh, my heavens!" Dottie screamed. "Now you've really done it!"

"Done what? He's the one that laid a hand on me first."

She knelt beside her dazed cousin. "Delbert! Delbert! Are you all right!"

The big oaf groaned, and his father came charging up the aisle with an iron skillet clenched in one hand and a new butcher knife in the other. "What have you done!"

"I've taught your son a lesson in manners," Longarm replied, massaging a bruised knuckle.

"Get out of my store before I beat your brains out or cut your throat."

Longarm took a step back. "You take a swipe at me with either one of those and I'll send you to the doctor— or the undertaker."

Iverson backed off at those words. He threw the knife and skillet on the floor and then shouted, "Dorothy, you're responsible for this!"

"No, I—"

Iverson slapped her across the mouth so hard that the little woman staggered and would have fallen if Longarm hadn't grabbed and supported her.

"Just don't move," Longarm ordered, balling up his fists with every intention of knocking Iverson's fool head from his shoulders.

"No, please!" she cried, grabbing his arm and hanging on tight. "I'll be all right. Just—just go!"

"Dottie, you don't have to put up with either of these two men. It doesn't matter that they're your relatives. I can help you find a better job."

"I'm all right!" she cried with exasperation. "Stop trying to help me, and just go away and don't ever come back!"

Longarm could see that she was on the verge of hysterics. And even though her own lip had been smashed and was bleeding, Dottie knelt beside Delbert and tried to comfort him, which completely baffled Longarm.

"Miss Quigley," he said, "I don't understand you even a little bit, but I can see that I've made a mistake coming here. I won't do it again and I apologize for the trouble I've caused."

With that, Longarm turned on his heel and stomped up the aisle. He was so furious that, when he reached the pickle barrel, he toppled it sending a wave of dills and the stinking brine streaming across the floor. It gave him no small amount of satisfaction to hear Iverson screeching as if he'd just been castrated.

Longarm was still in a dark mood when he finished a big breakfast of pancakes, coffee, and bacon. He checked his Ingersoll pocket watch and saw that it was ten minutes after ten. He was sure that Wade ought to have returned to his office by now, and decided to go pay his friend a visit and see if they could figure out why Dottie Quigley was so afraid of her relatives, even to the point of accepting their physical and verbal abuse.

Then he saw Wade and Henry Tilson across the street exiting one of Goldstrike's more unsavory saloons. The two lawmen had apparently arrested a couple of gamblers and they must have had some trouble, because their prisoners were bloodied and disheveled.

"Hey, Wade!" Longarm called, forgetting about Dottie and hurrying across the street. "What happened?"

Wade said something to his deputy, who escorted the battered gamblers on down to the jail while he waited for Longarm to cross the street.

"Nothing but a couple of card cheats that were using marked decks."

"How did you catch them?"

"Henry and I were making our morning rounds when we got a complaint. We slipped unnoticed into the saloon, and they didn't see us watching while they worked as a team to clean the pockets of some miners. When their suckers finally got wise to their game and trouble was about to erupt, Henry and me stepped in and made the arrests."

"Let me see their marked decks," Longarm said. "I've always been amazed at how many ways it can be done."

Wade shook his head. "There was a fight and the decks were scattered. We didn't bother to collect them."

"But won't you need them for evidence when they go to trial?"

Wade laughed. "Custis, we don't even have a regular judge. Just a circuit man that passes through about once a month. And I'll be damned if I'm going to feed and shelter those two until then."

"No trial?"

"Of course not! This isn't the big city! Hell, the city fathers would likely dock my wages if I held people like that over until the judge arrived."

Longarm was confused. "Well, how do you sentence them?"

44

"We just fine them and turn 'em loose with a warning that the fine will double the next time they're caught and arrested. Some stay in town and go honest, but a lot of them just leave for greener pastures."

"I guess that makes sense."

"Of course it does!" Wade rubbed his own bruised knuckles. "I still enjoy a good fight after all these years."

"I don't," Longarm said, displaying his own knuckles.

"What happened?"

"I had to teach Delbert Iverson a lesson in manners."

"You whipped that big galoot?"

"Yeah, and I should have laid out his father as well." Longarm shook his head. "I can't understand why a girl as sweet and pretty as Miss Quigley would stick with a pair like that."

"Maybe she's not as sweet as you think."

Longarm blinked. "What is *that* supposed to mean?"

"Nothing. But you can't judge someone just from being with them a few minutes. Custis, I think you're making snap judgments about that girl based on her looks, which we both know can be damned deceiving."

"Maybe, but you haven't seen the fear in her like I have when Iverson or his son come close. There's something strange going on there, and I'd like to sort it out."

"I'll bet Iverson went crazy when you knocked Delbert down."

"Oh, he did, all right! He came at me with a skillet in one hand and a butcher knife in the other. I warned him off and he was smart enough to drop them, or I'd have drawn my gun and laid it across the side of his stupid head."

"They're a pair, all right," Wade agreed. "But you'll

45

be leaving soon enough and I'd appreciate it if you just stayed away from the whole bunch. I'll be catching grief from Iverson for a long time after you're gone.''

Longarm reluctantly nodded his head. "You're right. I'm just passing through, but damned if I can tolerate watching a lady like Miss Quigley be abused."

"Look," Wade said, "why don't we just go have a drink and put our troubles behind us? I'll buy."

"It's too early for that," Longarm said. "Why don't we go fishing?"

"I better not until this afternoon."

"Why not?" Longarm demanded. "If you've got enough time to drink, then you've got enough time to fish."

"Look," Wade said with an edge of anger creeping into his voice, "*you're* the one on vacation, not me!"

"Forget it," Longarm said. "I'll go for a walk and spend some time with Rebecca."

"She'd like that. Just don't let her talk you into thinking that things aren't okay in Goldstrike and that I'm not happy."

"Are you?"

Wade snorted. "What kind of fool question is that? And what does being happy have to do with being a lawman—and soon a father?"

"I don't know about the father part, but a man has to enjoy his work."

"Well, I do! It's just that it don't pay very well and there's a lot of aggravation. Like right now when I find out you beat the hell out of Delbert and threatened his father. That's going to cost me some grief."

"Sorry I defended Miss Quigley and myself," Longarm snapped before he turned and headed on up the street. It was better to walk away from Wade when he got like that than try to reason with him. Was now, always had been.

"Custis!"

He inwardly groaned. "Hi, Gazella."

She pushed in close. "I don't know about you, but my butt is blistered. How about yours?"

"It's the same. Gazella, if you don't mind, you need to excuse me because I have things to do."

She was hurt. He could see that and felt bad, but he simply was not in the mood to be sociable or randy, either one.

"I thought we did something pretty special yesterday," she said.

"We did," he agreed, "but I just got into a row with the Iversons and then with Wade, and I'm feeling a little out of sorts at the moment."

"I could change that."

"Maybe you could," he said.

"I'll meet you up at the old fishing hole in one hour. How about it?"

He wanted to say no, but Gazella was wearing a low-cut dress and his eyes seemed to be drawn to her bosom like iron to a magnet.

"You want to do it again, don't you?" she asked.

"Yes," he told her, feeling disappointed because he was so weak when it came to this sort of thing.

"I thought so." She boldly leaned in close and kissed his lips and stroked his crotch, all in one swift but effective move. "See you soon!"

He shook his head and continued up the street. He decided to go for a walk because he didn't want to visit Rebecca and have her find out what he meant to do for most of the afternoon.

● ● ●

47

Longarm's butt was even more sunburned the next morning when he gently eased down at the kitchen table and Rebecca poured him a cup of coffee, then laid a platter of eggs and biscuits down none too gently.

"Well, Romeo," she said, "I hear that you have been quite busy."

Longarm groaned inwardly. She must have found out about the wild humping that he'd been having with Gazella the last two afternoons.

"Uh, what do you mean?"

"I mean everyone in town is talking about how you beat up Delbert Iverson and threatened his father."

"I didn't beat him up," Longarm said. "I defended myself and a certain young lady."

Rebecca's eyebrows arched in question. "Oh? Well, the way I heard it, you nearly killed Delbert. For sure you broke every one of the toes in the foot you stomped. It's going to be a while before he can even work in his father's store."

"He asked for it. And his father slapped Miss Quigley."

Rebecca's expression changed. "He hit her?"

"That's right. Broke one of her lips."

"I'm sorry. I never heard a thing said about Iverson hitting that young woman."

"Do me a favor," Longarm said. "Try and strike up a friendship with Dottie. She's living in fear, and I want to know why."

"Maybe she's just not a very strong person."

"Maybe," Longarm said, "but that isn't the impression I get. I think that something is happening that needs to be changed. I think that the Iversons are holding something over that young woman."

Rebecca frowned. "Perhaps it is something that you

really don't want to know about, Custis. I'm not saying that she has done something terrible in Utah or wherever she came from and is scared to death of being caught—but that might be the case.''

''Could be.''

''And if so, perhaps we would be smart just to stay out of her past altogether.''

''I'd agree, except that Delbert and his father are violent men and I've seen her abused and berated. If they treat her like that in front of the public, imagine how they must treat her when no one else is around.''

''I see what you mean,'' Rebecca said, dipping her chin in agreement. ''But you're not going to be here very long, and I'm not exactly in the best shape to be out and about.''

''I'm sorry,'' he said, embarrassed by his oversight. ''Maybe I can find someone else to—''

''You couldn't and shouldn't,'' Rebecca interrupted. ''And the very *last* person in Goldstrike that you should ask for help is Gazella.''

Longarm felt his cheeks blush as hot as his behind. ''I, uh . . .''

''Don't say a word, Custis. The truth is written all over your face.''

''You've made me feel ashamed of myself.''

''Why? I'm the one that encouraged you to make that woman's acquaintance. I just didn't know very much about her until the last day or two. As it turns out, she has more than one business operation in this town.''

Longarm fumbled for a cigar and lit it, then said, ''I guess I'd better walk off a ways seeing as how I know you hate the smell of these things.''

''Smooth exit,'' she said dryly. ''And I'll go pay Miss Quigley a visit tomorrow. If I do say so myself, I have quite a knack for getting people to open up about themselves.''

"So I've noticed.''

"And what about Henry Tilson?''

"I'm working on that,'' Longarm promised.

"Then we're working to help each other,'' Rebecca said with a smile, ''and that's the way it should be among dear friends.''

Chapter 5

Rebecca was feeling as big as a cow when she waddled into Iverson's general store the next afternoon and smiled at the proprietor. "I'm sorry to hear about what happened to your son yesterday. How is he feeling?"

"How would you feel with every toe on one of your feet crushed?"

"Well," Rebecca replied, "that is a shame, but then again, I understand that Delbert keeps bullying that new girl. What is her name?"

"Dorothy, and my boy never bullied her. She's just plain damned lazy! I have to keep after her every minute of the day just to get her to work. Del is just doing the same, that's all. I'm sorry I ever took her in, and I'm ready to send her back where she came from."

"Where's that?" Rebecca asked, already knowing.

"Utah Territory," Iverson snapped. "She's Mormon."

"Oh, I see. Well, perhaps she just needs to make new friends and get out in the town a little more. When my baby comes, I'm going to need help. Perhaps she could come and work for me part time."

"She wouldn't want to do that," Iverson replied,

shaking his head with a finality that Rebecca found very irksome. "And anyway, you wouldn't be any happier with Dorothy than I am. Besides, what am I supposed to do with Delbert laid up with five broken toes!"

"I have no idea."

"Well, how's this for an idea," Iverson hissed, pointing a finger at Rebecca's face. "I'm going to have that man arrested and sent to prison!"

"I don't think that is a very good idea."

"Why? Because he's your friend?"

"And a United States deputy marshal on vacation from Denver."

Iverson's jaw dropped and then his face reddened with anger. "So you're in cahoots with that bully. Well, I suppose that no judge would put him in prison, but you can tell him if he ever sets foot back in this store, I'll put a bullet through his belly."

Rebecca had to struggle in order not to lose her temper. "That would be a very, very foolish thing to do, and one that would most likely get you hanged."

"I'm on the city council," Iverson said, "and damned if I'll support your husband for reappointment."

"He doesn't need your support," Rebecca said tightly. "And as for that son of yours, couldn't he just sit on a stool up here by the cash register and finally be useful?"

"Del has trouble with numbers. He's a hard worker but he don't like figures and paperwork."

"Then perhaps Dorothy—"

"No!" The storekeeper lowered his voice. "I wouldn't trust that girl any farther than I could throw her handling my money. If she didn't cheat me, she'd cheat the customers, and then I'd be in an even worse fix than I am right now.''

"Mr. Iverson, if the girl is that lazy and dishonest, why don't you fire her?''

"It ain't that simple. Now, can I help you find something to buy or did you just want to waste my time with talk?''

"I'll buy something here when Hell freezes over,'' Rebecca snapped. "Right now I insist on meeting that young woman and asking if she's interested in helping me with my newborn.''

"I told you she's no good!''

"Why don't you let *me* be my own judge of her character and ability. Where can I find her?''

"She's off eatin' her dinner.''

"Out back by your loading area?''

"I—I don't think so.''

"Why don't I find out,'' Rebecca suggested, starting down the aisle.

"It's time she was back here and workin'! That girl ain't got time to talk.''

Rebecca ignored Iverson. The storeroom was open, and she saw the young woman sitting trancelike on a box, gazing forlornly at the alley.

"Miss Quigley?''

She started badly, then recovered. "Yes?'' she asked.

"I'm Mrs. Crockett, the marshal's wife. Can I speak to you a minute?''

"I don't know,'' Dottie answered. "I should be getting back to work. And maybe you ought to be home restin', ma'am.''

"I wondered if you could help me out a little with housework and the baby after it arrives,'' Rebecca blurted out, getting right to the point of her visit. "My husband works long hours and can't be around very much in the day or evening, and I really could use some help. I couldn't pay you much, but it would include the meals you cooked.''

"I'd like that, but my uncle wouldn't, so I'll have to say no."

"You could work when you're not working here."

Dottie wrung her hands in her lap. "I—I better not."

Rebecca came over and sat down beside the young woman. She felt weak and a little dizzy from the heat and her long walk. "I'm feeling a mite faint."

"You shouldn't be here," Dottie told her. "Your poor head could start spinning and you might fall and hurt yourself and the baby. I sure wish you hadn't come, Mrs. Crockett."

"Rebecca. Call me Rebecca."

"Yes, ma'am. My name is Dorothy, but you can call me Dottie."

"All right then," Rebecca said. "Why can't you accept my offer of part-time employment. Don't you like babies?"

She beamed. "Oh, that's not it at all. I love 'em! It's just that I agreed to stay close to work here at the store and my uncle, he wouldn't approve, especially with Del all hobbled up now."

"Dottie, in case you haven't heard, the Civil War is over and slavery has been abolished."

"I heard. But where I come from a woman obeys a man. And I got no rights here."

"Nonsense! You've got the right of freedom to choose where you work and how you spend your own time. I don't understand you at all."

Dottie pursed her lips in tight concentration for several moments before saying, "I was raised by Mormons and so I think different."

"Are you of their faith?"

She jumped to her feet. "I'd better get to work now. I'll help you up to the front and then you need to stay home and rest. When is your baby due?"

"At any time. Dottie, are you a Mormon?"

"Not anymore."

"What—"

But before she could finish, Dottie was taking her arm and gently moving her toward the door and then up the aisle saying, "I can't say no more, Mrs. Crockett! Now you go straight home and rest!"

"I will," Rebecca said, not sure how much she'd learned or accomplished, except that Custis was right—the girl was terrified of Mr. Iverson and his son. And that fact alone made Rebecca all the more determined to uncover her past and present secrets.

Longarm had been buying some ammunition in a gunsmith's shop across the street when he saw Rebecca emerge from the general store with Dottie at her arm. The two young women spoke for a moment. Then Iverson stepped out onto the boardwalk and shouted something, causing Dottie to cringe and then dash back inside. It made Longarm furious to see how that pretty gal jumped like a puppet every time Iverson pulled her string, and he wondered if she lacked courage.

No matter, because he could see that Rebecca was looking pale and peaked, so he hurried across the street and helped her to safety. "I shouldn't have asked you to go there," he said, guessing that she was extremely upset. "You're angry and worn out."

"I have an intense dislike for that awful man! Do you

55

know that he actually threatened to have you arrested and sent to prison for defending his niece?"

"That doesn't surprise me."

"And then he told me that he will try to get my husband fired and certainly won't support his appointment."

"I guess I've caused you and Wade some big problems."

"Never mind that! There are very few people in Goldstrike who can tolerate Iverson. If he didn't have the best selection and lowest prices in town, he'd have already gone under."

Longarm helped the woman back up the street to her home. "No more of that," he said, easing Rebecca into her favorite rocking chair. "But I have to ask if you found out anything about why that girl is so damned scared."

"She wouldn't actually say, but I have a feeling it goes beyond her uncle and cousin."

"What do you mean?"

"I have a feeling her fear has something to do with the Mormons. She might be a runaway, Custis."

"You mean someone's wife?"

"Yes. Or perhaps Dottie was being forced to marry a polygamist and went on the run."

Longarm could see that this might very well be at the root of the young woman's predicament. "Yes, but either way, Miss Quigley is free to make her own life now. Polygamy is against the law and so she'd not be legally married in Colorado."

"You need to explain that to her as soon as possible."

"I will."

"But stay out of the store," Rebecca warned, "because Iverson is just crazy enough to shoot you."

"There are other general stores. I came up here to go

fishing, but I'm not getting much of that done.''

"Perhaps Wade will get off early and you can go later this afternoon.''

"That would be nice.'' Longarm frowned with concern. "You look as if you need a nap, Rebecca. Why don't you go inside and lie down.''

"Are you worried about me, or have you got the buxom Miss Gazella West on your mind?''

Longarm blushed deeply, then barked a strained laugh. "Gazella has about worn me out. I guess maybe I'll take a nap of my own.''

Once he had Rebecca taken care of, Longarm went into the spare bedroom and took off his shoes. He stretched out on the bed and was soon snoozing. Later in the afternoon, he got up and pulled on his boots thinking he might get a haircut and shave, then go see if Wade wanted to go fishing. He might also keep an eye on the mercantile and try to catch Dottie leaving, then follow and talk to her about her troubles.

When Custis entered Wade's office, Deputy Tilson was gone, and so were the two battered gamblers he'd seen being escorted under arrest down the boardwalk. Longarm looked at the empty cell, then at his old friend, and said, "Justice is swift in Goldstrike.''

"Huh?''

"The two card cheats are already free.''

"Oh,'' Wade said, dropping a pair of handsome new boots off his desk. "Yeah, we let them go with a warning.''

"No fine for a marked deck or for putting up a fight against you and your deputy?''

"That's right. They . . . they were busted.''

"I see.'' Longarm didn't see. Not really. But he let

the matter drop and managed a smile. "How about we go fishing this afternoon."

"I'd enjoy that. Yeah. In fact, why don't we go right now? I can lock up and Henry will be back pretty soon."

"Great! I hope we're as lucky as we were a couple of days ago."

Wade grinned. "I hear that you've been dipping your pole in more than Crystal Creek, old friend."

"What do you mean?"

"Gazella." Wade burst into laughter. "Do you really think that anything goes unnoticed in this small a town?"

"I . . . ah . . ."

"You don't have to say a word. I just wanted you to know that everyone knows what is going on up at the old fishing hole."

"Now wait a minute."

"Custis, don't try to talk your way out of it because it won't do no good. Between whipping Delbert Iverson and romping on the wet sand with Gazella, you're the biggest news in Goldstrike. I swear that you're already a local hero!"

"Shut up, and let's go fishing," Longarm ordered with disgust as he headed out the door feeling as though every eyeball in this mining town was peeking out at him and watching his every move.

Chapter 6

"Dottie?" he shouted, overtaking her a block from Iverson's general store late that afternoon. She turned, and Longarm thought she was going to bolt and run. "Don't hurry off. I only want to talk to you for a moment."

"If they see me with you, I'm going to be in terrible trouble. Ever since you broke Delbert's toes it's been awful, and I don't want things to go from bad to worse."

"Why don't you quit and go to work for Rebecca? She really needs someone to stay with her."

Dottie looked up and down the street, then retreated between two buildings where she would be less conspicuous. "Don't you understand that I can't help anyone except myself right now? How many ways do I have to explain that to you?"

"You haven't even explained it one way so far," Longarm answered. "Dottie, I can't for the life of me figure out why you stay with the Iversons if you are so afraid."

"Marshal Long, that isn't any of your business!"

He stepped closer. The young woman was so desirable that Longarm wanted to put his arms around her, but he was sure that she would resist and then he'd never be able to help her.

"Listen, Rebecca is one of the nicest people in the world. Is it so much to ask that you help her and yourself at the same time?"

"I just can't," Dottie said, her eyes starting to glisten with tears. "I'd like to, but Mr. Iverson wouldn't approve."

"He's not your master." It was all that Longarm could do to keep from letting her hear the exasperation that he felt inside. "Dottie, I'm a United States deputy marshal and I can help if you will just tell me what is wrong!"

"I'm in trouble," she blurted out. "Big trouble. But if you fully understood, I'd likely be in even worse trouble. So . . ."

"Are you running away from polygamists?"

Her eyes widened. "How . . ."

"That's it," Longarm said, knowing he'd hit on the truth because of the sudden alarm in her dark brown eyes. "Dottie, you need to understand that Mormons have no power or authority over you in Colorado."

"You don't know them very well or you wouldn't say that."

"I've met plenty of Mormons. For the most part, they are good people, but there are bad just like with anyone else. I've known more than few polygamists and I don't like most of them, but they are not outlaws and they take good care of their large families."

"Custis, they think altogether different from you and don't recognize federal authority." Dottie shook her head. "They make their own laws and strictly live by them. And as for this being Colorado, that doesn't mean a thing to them."

"They have to abide by both federal and local laws."

"But they place Brigham Young's rules above all others, even federal law!'' Dottie shook her head. ''Oh, being a federal marshal, they might tell you what you want to hear ... until you're out of sight, and then they'll do whatever they please or what pleases their church.''

''I know that,'' Longarm replied. ''I also know that they're a hardworking, strong-willed people and not easily reasoned with when confronted with laws that contradict their religious beliefs. But that doesn't mean *you* have to be one of their followers and ruled by them.''

''I'm not one of them anymore. But once you have been, it is not easy to leave. I ... well, no matter. I've said more than I should.''

''What about Rebecca?''

''Can't she find someone else?''

''No,'' Longarm said. ''Not a woman that could be right there close if something suddenly goes wrong. And you have seen many children born, haven't you?''

Dottie reluctantly nodded. ''I'm no midwife, but I'd know exactly what to do if there were complications.''

''Then you really can't refuse,'' Longarm reasoned. ''And besides, you'll be paid.''

''I could use some extra money. But what would people say with you staying there too?''

''I'll be leaving very soon,'' Longarm told her.

''That's not good enough.''

''All right, then don't move in with the Crocketts but just visit, help with the baby, and do some cooking and cleaning after your work at the general store.''

''No,'' Dottie said with an emphatic shake of her head. ''You see, if I took up Rebecca's offer, my uncle and cousin Delbert would make my life a living hell.''

''Then come stay at the Crocketts.''

''And what about you? It's a small town and a small

61

house. I know how hurtful wagging tongues can be.''

Longarm appreciated her concern, and knew it was legitimate, so he said, ''I'll move into a hotel.''

''You'd do that?''

''Sure! Rebecca is exhausted and I'd do most anything to help her and make certain that she has an easier time than she's having now. I'll even supplement what she can pay you until she is well enough to handle things without help.''

''You are a very good friend. But—''

''You could leave the Iversons right now,'' he blurted out, cutting off her argument. ''I'll help carry your belongings over to the Crocketts' house.''

''I'm so worried!''

''I'll be around.''

''But you don't know my uncle and Delbert! There's no telling what they might do in retaliation.''

''If they try anything, they'll go straight to jail or to prison. Come on, Dottie! You'll never have a better chance to get out of this mess than right now.''

''All right,'' she decided with a deep exhalation of breath. ''It's Saturday and they always go out to dinner. Maybe . . .''

''How long will it be before they leave?''

''Less than an hour,'' Dottie replied, looking hopeful for the first time. ''We live on the corner of Second and Pine Streets—it's the white house with yellow trim.''

''I can find that in minutes.''

''All right then, Custis, I'll be packed and waiting.''

''You won't be sorry!'' Longarm exclaimed. ''It'll be good for you and good for Rebecca.''

''I . . . I sure hope so,'' Dottie said, trying to hide her concern. ''You have no idea how possessive they are.

Especially Delbert, who treats me like . . . well, never mind.''

"Everything will turn out just fine,'' Longarm promised. "And don't forget that you'll be staying in the town marshal's house and helping his wife and soon his newborn child.''

"I've already thought of that. But is he really good friends with Deputy Tilson?''

"Why do you ask?''

"Just wondering,'' Dottie replied, quickly changing the subject and turning to leave.

"One hour,'' Longarm called.

"Yes!''

She was smiling when she left. A beautiful smile that made Longarm's heart skip a beat. And as he continued on down the street, he began to whistle a happy tune. He'd done it! Hooray for Dottie and hooray for dear Rebecca.

"Yahoo, Custis, honey!''

"Uh-oh,'' he whispered under his breath before collecting his thoughts and turning to see Gazella hurrying along to catch up with him.

"Darling, wasn't that little girl with the black hair the same timid little mouse that works for those awful Iversons?''

"Her name is Dorothy Quigley.''

"Now whatever did she have to say to a real man like you?'' Gazella asked, taking his arm and batting her eyelids.

"She's going to move in and help Mrs. Crockett with her baby.''

"Whatever for?''

"She was asked . . . by Rebecca.''

"Hmmm,'' Gazella mused aloud. "Why ever would

Mrs. Crockett want a little strumpet like that in her house?''

"She knows a few things about babies," Longarm said, feeling a sharp pang of irritation.

"Why, honey! That little thing isn't much more than a baby herself!'' Gazella pressed closer and slid her hand down Longarm's hard thigh. "Isn't that right?''

"She's . . . ah, small, all right."

"Hardly more than a little girl, I'd say."

Longarm didn't agree, but this was not the time or the place to argue the point. He momentarily considered telling Gazella the rest of the story—that Dottie was going to come and stay with the Crocketts for a while until their baby was at least a few weeks old and Rebecca was strong enough to handle things by herself. But with Gazella now running her fingers over his pants and his manhood starting to swell, he figured that this was probably not the right time.

"Honey, you *are* in need of me," Gazella whispered, dropping her eyes to the bulging betrayal in his pants. "You want to go up and put your big old pole in our sweet little fishing hole?''

She giggled and jabbed him damned hard in the ribs, causing Longarm to take a sharp breath and pull back. "Gazella, you'll have to excuse me but I've got some things I have to do this afternoon."

"Oh?''

She waited for a further explanation, which Longarm wasn't about to volunteer. So after a long and strained silence, Gazella shrugged and said, "Well, big boy, there are plenty of big, hungry fish in this little pond called Goldstrike.''

He could tell that Gazella was steaming on the inside even though she was grimly smiling on the outside.

"Maybe tomorrow I'll go fishing," he said, wanting to take back the words as soon as they were out of his mouth.

"Fine!" Gazella's smile widened. "Shall we say about this time tomorrow?"

"Okay."

She kissed his cheek and tried to nibble on his ear, but Longarm turned his head and eased back out of range. "I . . . I won't be staying here much longer."

"When are you leaving, honey?"

She looked genuinely sad, and so he shrugged. "Might not be for a few days yet."

"I've been thinking of making a little trip down to Denver to see the latest fashions. Maybe . . ."

Longarm knew what was coming and shook his head. "I have to stop by at Cripple Creek on the way back and take care of some law business."

"Too bad! We could have had a nice time traveling together. Perhaps we could meet in Denver in a couple of weeks?"

"Say," he said, "that might be just the thing. Well, I've got to go now."

"See you tomorrow at the old fishin' hole, and don't you dare forget to bring *our* favorite fishing *pole*." She giggled, waving all her chubby fingers.

Longarm was still muttering darkly about how weak he was when it came to the pleasures of the flesh. When he went to collect Dottie a short while later, she was standing on Iverson's front porch with a wicker suitcase clutched in one hand and a coat and gunnysack full of extra clothes in the other. She looked scared, but determined, and the mere sight of such a small, lovely, and brave creature erased his former sense of self-disgust.

"Oh," Dottie breathed when he took the gunnysack

and suitcase from her hand and started across the yard with her at his side, "I sure hope I'm not going to cause more trouble for you and the Crocketts than I'm worth."

"You won't," Longarm vowed. "Did you leave the Iversons a note of explanation, or do you just want me to come around later and give them the bad news?"

"Don't do that! There might be a gunfight!"

"I'm a federal marshal, remember? If they started slinging lead at me, they'd either be headed for prison or the cemetery."

Dottie gulped. "I don't want them killed!"

"Let's not talk about things that won't happen," Longarm said as they headed up the street toward Rebecca's house.

"Have you moved out yet?" she asked.

"No," Custis admitted.

Dottie stopped and looked up at him with her jaw set. "Well, I can't go there until you do!"

"I'll move out as you move in," he promised.

"You'd better! I don't have much of a reputation, but what I have I'd like to keep."

"I'd say that was the least of your worries, Miss Quigley."

"Yeah," she admitted with a sigh as they started walking again, "I guess you are right."

When they arrived at the Crockett house, Wade was still at work, but Rebecca met them on the front porch, and when she learned that she was going to have help, she was overjoyed. She hugged Dottie as best she could, given her size, and then turned to Longarm. "Custis, how on earth did you manage to change this girl's mind?"

"I don't know."

"He said that you really needed me," Dottie chimed

in. "And he got me to admit that I could be useful in birthing. So . . . well, here I am!"

"Does your uncle and Delbert know?" Rebecca asked.

Dottie's smile faded like grease on a hot griddle. "Not yet. But I did leave them a note and they'll be back pretty soon to read it. After that, well, I just hope they don't come hunting for me."

"If they do," Longarm growled, "they'll be making one hell of a big mistake."

"Maybe they won't," Dottie said, trying to sound hopeful. "With all his broken toes, Delbert don't like to move around very much. He never did anyway, but this has made him even worse."

Longarm went out on the front porch and plopped down in a rocking chair. "Why don't you ladies get settled and just toss my stuff out here on the porch. I'll find a hotel."

"You'll do nothing of the sort!" Rebecca cried.

"I have to," Longarm explained. "Otherwise, Dottie's reputation could be compromised."

"Hmmmph!" Rebecca snorted. "What you can do is sleep out here on the front porch. I'll bring bedding and you'll eat at our table until you're fished out and return to Denver."

"I'd like that," Longarm told her. "It'd work out just fine."

In actuality, he was thinking that if the Iversons were crazy enough to try to steal Dottie back, the porch was exactly where he'd most want to be when they arrived.

The Iversons never appeared, but Dottie was so nervous she couldn't eat a thing that evening. Wade came home about the time it got dark, and he wasn't as pleased about the new arrangement as Longarm had hoped.

"Now Iverson is going to raise hell," he said.

"Who the hell cares," Longarm growled as they settled in on the porch while the women got better acquainted inside.

"I care! I've got a wife, and soon a baby. Iverson isn't well liked, but he is respected and his voice carries a lot of weight in Goldstrike. He can influence the other members on the city council, and he has money enough to back candidates in the next election who'll kick me out."

"I'm sorry," Longarm said, offering his friend a cigar. "I've probably put my foot into something where it don't belong."

"Aw," Wade said, biting the tip off the cigar and spitting it into Rebecca's rose garden before lighting it, "never mind. I can't stand Iverson, and I have to say that I'm enjoying how you pulled his tail and now have stolen his niece."

"I didn't 'steal' her," Longarm said, lighting his cigar. "I just got her out of a bad fix."

"She tell you what *kind* of trouble she's in?"

"Rebecca had already guessed that she was running from a polygamist."

"She's married to one?"

"I didn't ask."

"She sure is young."

"They marry them off young," Longarm said. "I've seen child brides of thirteen and fourteen soon having babies."

Wade shook his head. "She sure is a pretty thing. Now that she's out from under Iverson's thumb, I'll bet there'll be a string of young bachelors banging on my door while she's here helping out."

"Wouldn't surprise me."

They talked until late into the evening, when the stars were out and the moon was a big silver wedge in the glittering sky. And they drank some brandy and each smoked another cigar. All in all, it was the best visit that Longarm had had with his friend, and when Wade went to bed, Longarm dragged out some blankets and was more than happy to sleep on the porch. It was a beautiful night, and since the altitude was so high, the stars felt close enough so that a man could reach out and pluck them from the heavens, one by one.

Longarm guessed it must have been two or three o'clock in the morning when he awakened to the sound of a gunshot and the accompanying shatter of window glass. Inside, Rebecca screamed and Wade shouted hoarsely for her to stay down on the floor. Longarm rolled along the porch with his gun in his fist. But whoever had fired the bullet wasn't about to show himself.

"Them sonsabitches!" Wade shouted, coming outside wearing nothing but a flannel nightshirt. "How dare they—"

Wade didn't get to finish his sentence because another rifle shot shattered the night air. Wade grabbed his belly and went stumbling back through his doorway. Longarm was up and firing into the night before his friend hit the floor. He had turned to shout at Wade to stay down himself, but his warning had been a moment too late.

Rebecca shrieked again, and Longarm threw himself back inside and slammed the door.

"Oh, my God, no!" Rebecca cried, falling to her husband's side. "Please, no!"

Longarm knelt beside his friend. "Wade, just take it easy," he pleaded, ripping open the man's nightshirt, and then groaning with despair when he saw the bullet hole that had torn through Wade's gut.

His friend looked up at Rebecca and said, "I can't die now! I can't die without seeing my baby boy!"

Rebecca was a strong woman, but she went to pieces, and it was Dottie who grabbed a towel and tried to stop the bleeding.

"Who could have shot me?" Wade gasped, staring around the room wildly as if he might see his assassin. "Why would someone do this!"

"It must have been Iverson or his boy," Longarm answered. "But don't worry, I'll find out and by gawd they'll go swing!"

"You get 'em both!" Wade hissed, reaching up for Rebecca and then clutching her to his chest. "You take good care of my son and raise him right, hear me?"

"I hear you!" Rebecca sobbed. "Oh, Wade, maybe—"

"Shhh," he whispered, "I'm a goner. Ain't no doubt about it. I seen men shot not near as bad as me die. My belly is on fire and it's getting dark and cold already! Dammit to hell, it won't take long!"

Tears were also rolling down Dottie's cheeks, and she was trying to staunch the flow of dark blood, but it was no use, and Longarm grabbed her arm and said, "It's all right. Nothing we can do now but say a prayer for him."

"It's all my fault! If I hadn't come, this wouldn't have happened!"

"Girl," Wade wheezed, "it's not your fault and don't you dare blame yourself. You did nothing wrong and we hold nothing against you for this. I just . . . !"

With a strangled sound way down in his throat, Wade

stiffened and his eyes grew round and wide.

"No!" Rebecca screamed.

His bloodless lips moved soundlessly, and then he shuddered and was gone.

Rebecca went crazy, and Dottie held her tight. Longarm rushed outside; by now there were neighbors standing around with lanterns in their fists and wanting to know what had happened.

"It's your marshal," Longarm told them as he tore a lantern from someone's hand and went to see if all the killer's tracks had been destroyed by these morbid curiosity-seekers. "Someone ambushed him. He's dead."

There was a soft, communal groan, and Longarm regretted the harshness of his words because it was clear they felt terrible at this devastating news.

"Any idea who did it?" a silhouette asked.

"Yes!"

"Well?"

"Go home," Longarm ordered, hearing Rebecca's wails in the night. "Go home and say your prayers for a man who gave his life for this town and got damned little in repayment."

They all left then, and Longarm finished his search for clues, finding none, as expected. Then he went back to the house, sat down for a minute, and tried to pull himself together. He started to shake a little, and realized that it had been a long, long time since anyone's death had hit him so hard. Not as hard as poor Rebecca, but fist-hard in the belly so that he felt like vomiting all his grief.

But he couldn't. All he could do was try to stay close to Rebecca for a while, and then go pay a visit to the

Iversons. He'd have no evidence to arrest them, and really no jurisdiction. The authority, damn it to hell, would now belong to Henry Tilson. And that was a tragedy, in and of itself.

Chapter 7

It was a long, long night and Rebecca was inconsolable. Nothing was said about making funeral arrangements or what the future might hold for Rebecca and the now-fatherless child she was about to deliver into this world. Dottie was a godsend. Though small and only in her early twenties, she displayed great strength and compassion. She and Longarm both took turns holding Rebecca until after dawn.

"What are we going to do without Wade?" Rebecca whispered as the sun came up the next morning. "What on earth can we do?"

"You'll do all right," Longarm assured the woman. "I think that you ought to come back to Denver with me. I'll rent, maybe even buy a little house and take care of you and the baby until you can sort things out and decide what you want to do."

"I don't know," Rebecca said, looking dazed and drawn. "The thought of leaving everything including Wade is too hard to bear."

"I can understand a little of that," Dottie told her. "But maybe in a week or so, you'll have a clearer idea of what is best for you and the baby."

"By then, I'll *have* my husband's baby!" Rebecca cried fresh tears.

It broke Longarms's heart to see the depth of her grief, and what he really wanted to do was to go arrest the Iversons. If they ran, he'd find them, but he did not think they would run. He had thought a lot about what might have happened last night on the porch, and the most likely explanation was that Delbert was the probable assassin. It seemed entirely possible that he'd really meant to kill Longarm for breaking his toes, humiliating him in front of Dottie, and then stealing her away last evening. That made the most sense. Old Man Iverson would have been furious too, but he was wiser and had more to lose than gain by killing Longarm. Maybe they'd done it together, but that seemed unlikely.

"I'm leaving for a while," Longarm said about six o'clock that morning.

The two women both looked up, but it was Dottie who asked the question. "Where?"

"Who's the undertaker?"

Rebecca took a deep breath. "His name is Elias Mason. He's a friend and has probably already heard about my husband's death. I expect he will be along on his own."

"All right then," Longarm said, looking at Dottie. "I'm going to pay a visit to the Iversons. I think Delbert probably shot Wade by mistake."

Dottie must have reached the same conclusion. "He'll fight arrest. He carries a gun and he knows how to use it."

"Well, so do I!" Longarm lowered his voice. "What about your uncle?"

"I don't know," she said, looking down at Wade's body. "But if I had to guess, he wasn't part of this."

74

"Why not?"

"He's not sneaky like Delbert. It wouldn't be like him to ambush someone. He'd try to kill them face-to-face."

"All right then," Longarm said. "I'll be back later."

Rebecca came over and hugged his neck. "Maybe you should stay here and let Deputy Tilson arrest Delbert. That way—"

"No," Longarm said abruptly. "He might even refuse for lack of evidence, or because he wants to be the next marshal and wouldn't want to cross Iverson."

Rebecca nodded, but her eyes showed no comprehension, so Longarm pulled on his hat, checked his gun, and left.

"Custis!"

Longarm halted by the front gate.

"Custis, you watch out for Delbert," Dottie said. "He carries a knife as well as a gun and he's awful strong."

"Where is his knife?"

"In his right boot."

"Thanks."

"If Rebecca comes to Denver with you . . . could I come too? I don't want to leave her with the baby."

"Sure you can. Just—just try and get her through the birthing, Dottie. I know this won't make things any easier."

"We spoke about that," Dottie said, laying her hand on his sleeve. "Rebecca feels that the child she carries is Wade's legacy. His gift to her. She hopes it is a boy, but a girl will be just fine."

"What do you think about all of this?" Longarm asked.

"It's awful! The possibility that I might be the cause of Mr. Crockett's death makes me feel terrible."

"I can understand that, but remember Wade's dying

words. He didn't blame you and he pleaded that you not blame yourself. Don't let those final words be in vain, Dottie. Keep remembering them.''

"I'll try.'' She threw her arms around his waist and hugged him tightly, and Longarm felt her shoulders shaking as she silently wept.

"This sadness will pass,'' he said.

"I don't think so. Not for Rebecca anyway.''

"You're wrong,'' Longarm told her. "In time, she'll find someone new to love. And there will be periods when she feels a passing sadness for Wade. For the fact that he never got to see his only child. But she'll have a new life and new hopes. Rebecca is strong, like you.''

"And you.'' Dottie looked up at him, tear tracks running down her pretty cheeks. "Don't think we can't understand how much you loved your friend. Rebecca and I talked about that last night too.''

"When?''

"You fell asleep for a few minutes. Custis, I'm sorry for you too!''

He hugged her, and then headed down the street. People were out in their yards already, and as he plodded past their houses they called out sad greetings. Longarm did not acknowledge them, for his mind was now focusing on the Iversons. When he arrived at their house he reached across his waist and drew his pistol, then marched right up to the door, watching the windows to make sure that Delbert or his father did not suddenly open fire and kill him on the spot.

Kicking the door over and over with the toe of his boot, Longarm shouted. "Come on out! You are both under arrest!''

"Go to hell!'' Delbert shouted from somewhere inside the house.

76

Longarm tried the door handle and found it locked. He stepped back and shot the handle off, then kicked in the door and jumped back sideways, avoiding three gunshots. Everything in him wanted to jump back into the doorway and open fire, but he knew that was a good way to die, so he waited.

"You're under arrest for the murder of Marshal Wade Crockett!"

"He didn't kill him!"

Longarm recognized Iverson's voice. "He's still under arrest for just trying to shoot me, a United States deputy marshal! Tell him to throw down his gun and come out with his hands up! You do the same!"

"I tell you, neither one of us killed Crockett!"

"We'll see about that," Longarm replied. "Now are you coming out standing up—or down and dead!"

"Just a minute!" Iverson cried. "For gawd sake, give us a minute or two!"

"You got one damn minute!"

Longarm started counting to sixty. He could hear the two men arguing in a back room and then shouting at each other. When he reached the count of sixty, Longarm yelled, "That's it! Time is up! What's it going to be!"

Suddenly, he heard a dull thud followed by a body crashing to the floor. It was a sound he'd often heard. Then Iverson screamed, "My son is unconscious! Don't shoot! For the love of gawd, please don't kill us!"

"Throw out the guns!"

Two pistols came flying out the door, and Longarm collected them before he stepped inside. He was slightly familiar with the front room, for he'd seen it from the outside only the day before when he'd collected Dottie and her gunnysack and suitcase of belongings. But the shades were now drawn and it was very dim inside, so he crouched low and leveled his gun at the back hallway.

"Drag your son out right now!"

"I—I can't! He's too big and I got a bad back."

"Then come out with your hands over your head, and you'd better not be playing any games or I'll put a bullet in you faster than you can blink."

Iverson came out. He was fully dressed, and although Longarm couldn't distinguish his features clearly, the man's posture indicated that he was tired and defeated.

"Come on!" Longarm snapped.

When the older man reached him, Longarm grabbed him by the shirt and hurled him outside into the yard. He jumped on the man's back, put his gun to Iverson's head, and warned, "If you move even a damned muscle while I'm inside, I'll come back out and kill you."

"You got no right!"

"You're wrong! I've got a badge and the law on my side. Now shut up, or I'll shut you up!"

Longarm jumped up and looked around to see neighbors gawking. "Everyone go back inside! There could be gunplay yet and you don't want to catch a wild bullet!"

They vanished, and Longarm went into Iverson's house fast and low, thinking that this still might be a trick. But Delbert was down and he was unconscious. There was blood pooling on the floor, and Longarm knelt by the man's side and took his pulse. It was weak and racing. Delbert was alive but his father, probably out of panic, had struck him much too hard.

"Damn!" Longarm swore to himself, then holstered his gun before grabbing and dragging the young man outside on the porch and yelling, "Get up! You hit him too hard!"

Iverson moaned and rushed to his son's side. When he saw Delbert's lack of color and all the blood, he twisted around and threw up on his porch, then began to sob hysterically.

Henry Tilson came running up to the house all out of breath and half dressed. "What the hell is going on!"

"Figure it out," Longarm hissed.

"Jaysus, Long, did you brain the kid?"

"No, his father did."

Tilson's gaze swiveled back and forth from father to son and he said, "We better get Old Man Barker. He's the closest thing to a doc we got and he—"

"It's too late," Longarm said. "This one just died."

Iverson had been retching, but when he heard this news he howled and tried to tear Longarm's gun from its holster and kill him. He almost succeeded too. The man's grief was genuine and he was insane with fury. It took everything Longarm had left to overpower the store owner and force him into submission.

"Deputy Tilson, arrest this man," Longarm ordered.

"*Marshal* Tilson. And what are the charges?"

"You know what they are unless you were passed out all last night. Dammit, arrest him for the murder of Marshal Crockett!"

"On what evidence?"

Longarm jumped to his feet and drew his gun. He jammed it into Tilson's gut, stared into his bloodshot eyes, and smelled the man's whiskey-stinking breath before saying, "Is *this* evidence enough for you!"

Tilson nodded, eyes dropping down to the gun punched into his belly. "Ease up, man! I . . . I feel bad about Wade dyin' too! But . . ."

"No talk," Longarm spat. "Later, but not right now. I'm going into that house and I'm going to find the rifle that killed Wade. I'm going to smell the fresh gunpowder and we're going to have a trial here when the circuit judge comes around.''

"But maybe it was Delbert that killed Wade!''

"Maybe, but until we find out for sure, this man stays in jail. Is that understood?''

Tilson dipped his chin. "Yeah. Yeah. Take it easy. Just calm down.''

Longarm shoved Tilson aside without a word and went into Iverson's house. He would find the rifle if it meant tearing the floor up and even the walls. Either Delbert or his father was responsible, and there was still a debt to be paid.

"Well,'' Tilson said, looking up from Wade's desk where he now sat scowling. "Did you find the rifle?''

"No.''

"Then you ain't got shit! I could be holding an innocent man here!''

"Too bad,'' Longarm said, glancing over at the jail cell. "He may not be the one that pulled the trigger, but I'll guarantee you he was in on the ambush.''

"You're crazy!'' Iverson screamed.

Longarm rushed over to the cell, and had it not been locked, he would have grabbed the older man and beaten him senseless if he hadn't gotten a confession. But the cell was locked, so he just gripped the bars and said, "You or your son hid the rifle someplace outside the house. I'm going to put up a hundred-dollar reward and someone will find it!''

"How you gonna know it's even my rifle!'' the old man cried. "Marshal Tilson, you got to protect me from this crazy man! Isn't it enough that I killed my own son? How much do I have to suffer?''

"Long," Tilson said, "he's right. How would you know that it *was* their rifle?"

"Someone would recognize it."

"No! He *sells* all kinds of used rifles and handguns outta that general store. Didn't you see 'em?"

Longarm shook his head.

"Well, he does. The whole town knows it. Finding a rifle out there somewhere don't mean anything!"

Longarm clenched the cell bars until his knuckles were white, and then he shook them with all his strength. Finally, he looked at Iverson, who had retreated to the back of the cell, and hissed, "I'll find a way to prove you and your son killed my best friend. So help me God, if it takes the rest of my life, I'll see that you go to Hell!"

"I'm already there," Iverson replied, burying his face in his hands and weeping.

Longarm spun on his heels and headed outside, but Tilson's words stopped him cold. "I'm the law in Goldstrike. Not you! You got no right to badger that man. No right at all. I got to turn him loose without evidence. You hear me, Mr. Federal Lawman?"

"I hear you," Longarm said, turning back to face Tilson. "And I want you to hear me. Get out of Wade's chair."

"Huh?"

"Get out of his chair!"

Tilson jumped to his feet.

"I see you in Wade's chair or at his desk again, I'll beat you to a nubbin and kick your lazy ass out the door."

Tilson gulped. "You can't do that."

"Don't test me," Longarm said in a voice that quivered with barely suppressed rage. "And if you let that man go free before I allow it, I might have to kill him in self-defense."

"What self-defense are you talking about!"

Longarm's smile was deadly. "My own."

"He's insane!" Iverson shrieked from his cell. "Marshal, you got to protect me or I'm a dead man!"

"He's right," Longarm vowed as he headed for the newspaper office. He would post a reward for information regarding the heinous murder of Marshal Wade Crockett. He would offer a hundred . . . no, a *two*-hundred-dollar reward, and keep raising it until he had a hangman's noose choking the neck of Wade's killer.

Chapter 3

It was a simple funeral, and Longarm couldn't remember
much about what was said at the grave as he stood grim-
faced supporting Rebecca, who seemed to be in a daze.
Dottie was helping too, and Longarm didn't know what
he'd have done without the Mormon girl. He no longer
cared about her mysterious past in Utah. She had left
the Iversons and come to help, and that was good
enough. If Dottie had inadvertently been the cause of
Wade's death, she was not to blame. All that mattered
to Longarm was that Rebecca delivered a healthy child
and went on to live a full life. That, and getting evidence
to either convict Iverson for murder or discover Wade's
real killer.

So far his two-hundred-dollar reward for the killer's
identity had not produced results. Tomorrow, he'd raise
the ante to three hundred dollars.

"And so, my children of God," the minister con-
cluded, "we lay to rest a good and courageous young
man gunned down in the very prime of his life, just days
before the birth of his first child. We draw comfort
knowing that Marshal Wade Crockett is now enjoying
the eternal joy of heaven. Amen."

Rebecca was weeping softly, and it was all that Longarm and Dottie could do to ease her through the somber crowd to a waiting funeral carriage.

"Marshal Long?" a man lacking any distinguishing features said, whispering so that he could barely be heard. "I got some information for that there reward money you are offerin'."

Custis surveyed the unkept man for a moment, and said, "Meet me back here in two hours."

"You gonna bring the cash?"

Longarm didn't answer, but instead helped the women into the carriage and then climbed in after them. His eyes were directed straight ahead, but he heard the rhythmic thud of dirt being pitched onto Wade's simple casket as they drove away.

He returned two hours later to find the grave neatly mounded and covered with bright wildflowers. The man who had asked about the reward was lounging on someone else's tombstone and spitting copious amounts of chewing tobacco on a tribe of red ants.

Longarm felt an immediate revulsion toward this stranger, but he had brought the reward money—just in case.

"What can you tell me?" he asked without wasting time on introductions.

"I know who shot your friend, Marshal Crockett," was the man's answer as he hopped off the tombstone, hitched up his beltless pants, and narrowed his eyes. "I can tell you and I can tell the judge too."

"Who fired the shots?"

He wagged his chin back and forth with a sly grin. "I ain't quite as dumb as I look. First you pay me the reward money, then I'll tell you the name of the killer."

"No deal," Longarm snapped. "You could tell me

anything and then take the money and run. I need proof.''

The man forked two dirty fingers to his close-set eyes. "The proof," he declared, "is right here in my head. I *seen* the man that shot Marshal Crockett. I seen him fire the bullet.''

"Is that right?''

"Yep. I just happened to be out enjoyin' the evenin' and I was passin' the Crockett house and then bang, bang, bang! And then the marshal fell over dead.''

Longarm pretended to be interested. "Three shots, huh?''

"I didn't have time to count. Could have been four, I guess. They came real fast and the marshal just slumped over and died pretty quick. It was a sad thing. Not right, what with his wife about to have a kid. Damned dirty thing, it was.''

"What's your name?''

"Huh?''

Longarm took a menacing step forward and repeated, "What is your name?''

"Irwin. Irwin Duggan. Why?''

"Well, Irwin," Longarm said, controlling his temper and disappointment. "There were only *two* shots fired, not three or four.''

"I told you they came fast and . . . and I'd been pullin' pretty hard on a bottle of Old Mountain whiskey that night. But I saw what happened and by gawd I want that high-and-mighty Mr. Iverson to hang!''

"He's the one?''

"I . . .'' Irwin cleared his throat. "I just give it away, didn't I? But I won't testify without that two hundred dollars reward money. No, sir! You said you'd pay and—''

Longarm grabbed Duggan by his shirtfront, hauled him up on his toes, and growled, "Get out of my sight and don't you ever let me see you again!"

"Let go of me!" the man cried in a panic. "I come to help and now you're tryin' to scare me into testifyin' without no money nor nothin'! Shoot, that's rotten."

Longarm pushed the man, who fell over a headstone, landed hard on his back, and then scrambled to his feet. Longarm took a couple of steps toward him, and Duggan turned and ran for town screaming, "You lawmen are all no damned good. Crockett was a cheat too! He and Tilson are worse'n crooks, by gawd, and I'll bet you're jest the same!"

Longarm started running after Duggan. He was lean and long-legged, and it didn't take much to overtake the smaller man and haul him up short.

"Don't kill me, Marshal!"

"I ain't gonna kill you. But you've got some explaining to do!"

Duggan's brown eyes rolled around like marbles in a jar, and there was the smell of fear in his cold sweat. "Okay, so I lied. I need the money."

"Everybody needs money."

Duggan began to shake. "Yeah, but I need a drink real bad."

"All right," Longarm said after a moment's consideration, "let's go find a bottle and a nice spot where we can talk without being overheard."

"You gonna buy me whiskey?" the man asked, suddenly looking hopeful instead of terrified.

"Yes."

"You gonna pay me for tellin' you somethin' about Marshal Crockett and his deputy?"

"I might, but you're not going to live long enough to

enjoy anything if you don't slow down on the whiskey.''

"I tried, but I can't stop."

"Yeah," Longarm said, "I've heard that a few times before."

He marched Duggan into the nearest saloon. The curious bartender sure looked like he wanted to ask questions, but Longarm's glare was so intimidating that he did not dare.

"All right," Custis said, bottle clenched in one fist and Duggan in the other. "Let's go find a nice, private spot to talk."

"Can I have a drink first?"

"No. Talk first, then drink."

Duggan was beginning to shake, but Longarm didn't care. He marched the drunk down the street and into an alley where they could not possibly be overheard.

"All right, tell about Marshal Crockett and Deputy Tilson. Tell me what they were doing wrong in Goldstrike."

"I . . ." Duggan licked his lips. "I didn't mean nothin', Marshal. I was angry about the reward and everything. I sure could use a drink but I was lyin' again, same as I do most all the time."

"No, you weren't," Longarm growled. "You were mad and telling the truth. I hate to say that, but I think you were and I want to know about it right now."

"What they were doin', you mean?"

"That's right."

"He was your friend. If I speak bad of Marshal Crockett, you might kill or beat the hell outta me."

"If you don't speak at all, I'll whip you for sure," Longarm lied.

Duggan licked his lips and stared at the bottle of whiskey, so Longarm gave him a taste, then pulled it back and ordered, "Start talking."

"They was shakin' down the whores and the gamblers for protection money," Duggan whispered, unwilling to meet Longarm's eyes.

"I don't believe it!"

Duggan cringed, expecting a blow. "I didn't think you would, but it is still the truth!"

"You don't know the meaning of the word."

"I can give you a name or two and maybe you'll believe *them*," Duggan gushed. "But . . . but I sure need another pull on that bottle first."

Longarm allowed it, and then said, "I want the names of the gamblers and prostitutes they were holding up for money."

"They'd just started," Duggan replied. "They roughed up a couple of gamblers last week. Beat hell outta 'em and then threw 'em in jail overnight until they agreed to pay. After the others saw that they'd get some of the same, they started payin' Tilson."

Longarm had a bad feeling in the pit of his belly that he might be hearing the truth this time. He remembered how driven Wade had seemed about getting more money so that his family could have a more comfortable life, especially if he were ever killed while on duty.

"You say they paid Deputy Tilson," Longarm replied. "How do you know that Marshal Crockett knew and approved?"

"Because he and Tilson went around together demanding money from the whores and gamblers! Everyone of them was gonna have to pay!"

"How much?"

Duggan shrugged. "How should I know? I ain't no cardsharp and I sure ain't no whore."

Longarm scowled. "I remember two gamblers that they arrested and brought to jail."

"Them's the two that I was talkin' about. They was all beat up, weren't they?"

"Wade said they'd resisted arrest."

"Resisted arrest my fanny! They just refused to pay what Crockett and Tilson were demanding for protection. Said that they'd been down on their own luck and couldn't afford to pay the house a cut and also the damned law."

"Which prostitutes were paying?"

"All of 'em," Duggan flatly stated. "They were real upset with the law and afraid to do anything about it. I heard . . . well, never mind."

"What did you hear?"

Duggan's bloodshot eyes came to rest on the bottle. "I been tellin' you the truth this time. I swear I have. I been tellin' you everything I know. How about a little more hair of the dog for old Irwin?"

Longarm let him drink. He was dazed by this new and sad revelation. How could Wade have sunk to extortion? Couldn't he have . . . What? Longarm asked himself bitterly.

"That's enough. Give me the name of a woman."

"You can take your pick. Tilson was the one that went around and told them all it was time to pay up or leave town on the run without a cent. Most paid 'cause they weren't askin' a whole lot of money. But everyone knew they'd get the shit beaten out of 'em if they refused, just like them two gamblers."

Longarm had interrogated hundreds of lying men and a few honest ones. Over the years, he'd learned to determine one kind from the other, and he knew Duggan was telling the truth.

"You gonna give me the two hundred dollars?"

"No."

"I didn't think you would." Duggan sighed. "What about the bottle of whiskey I been drinkin'?"

"I have a few more questions," Longarm replied, forcing himself back to the present and avoiding the thought of how he'd deal with this new discovery about Wade. "Any idea who killed Marshal Crockett?"

"No, but I don't expect it was either one of the Iversons."

"Why not?"

Duggan shrugged. "They wasn't being shaken down, was they?"

"I . . . I doubt it. But they had their reasons." Longarm did not tell the man that he still harbored the suspicion that *he* had been the assassin's real target.

"Old Man Iverson ain't so bad as he sounds. He's like a dog that growls but never bites."

"What about Delbert?"

"Now he *was* a bad one," Duggan admitted as hatred twisted his mouth. "Delbert was a mean bully. He used to tease me when I was passed out in the alley behind their store. One day, Marshal Crockett caught him twistin' my arm up behind my back and laughing in my face."

"What did Wade do?"

"He got real mad at Delbert and told him he'd whip his butt if he ever did that to me again. They yelled at each other and Delbert grabbed a shovel to use on Crockett, who drew his gun. I thought the marshal was goin' to shoot, and I believe he would have if Delbert hadn't dropped that shovel."

"Maybe he should have," Longarm said, relieved to hear about how his best friend had risked his neck and maybe even his career to help a lost soul like Irwin Duggan.

"Then why don't you think Delbert shot the marshal?"

"He couldn't hit the side of a barn if he was standing next to the damned thing!"

"Are you sure?"

"Of course I am! He was a terrible shot."

"Some shots are lucky."

"Not if it was Delbert shooting. Like I said, he was terrible with a pistol or rifle. He wouldn't have even tried to shoot Crockett. He'd have done something sneaky instead, like poisoning him or even stealing money from his pa to hire a real gunman."

"Maybe that's exactly what Delbert did."

"Maybe, but I doubt it," Duggan said. "If you ask me, it was a gambler or one of the whores that got mad about having to pay who ambushed the marshal. And they might shoot Tilson next."

"You got anything else to say?"

"I sure need some money. Even a couple of dollars would help."

Longarm produced ten dollars and held it up in front of the man's face. "I'm going to give you this to get a room, a bath, and some clean clothes."

"Why? I'll be drunk on the street by Sunday and it won't matter."

"It *will* matter," Longarm countered. "You do what I say and I'll pay you more if you can tell me more."

"You mean . . ."

"I mean like who *really* killed my best friend."

"I'll try to help you find out. Maybe it was Tilson because he wanted all the money."

"Now you're thinking," Longarm said. He gave the

man the money and the bottle, then headed back out on the street. Tilson was standing in front of the office, but he ignored Custis and then turned and walked away. Longarm's head was reeling from what he'd learned. He knew that he could never tell Rebecca that her husband had resorted to shaking down gamblers and prostitutes. Wade wasn't the first lawman to do such a thing, and he wouldn't be the last, but it was a sad and sorry business and one that left a very sour taste in Longarm's mouth.

Chapter 9

Longarm went in search of the two gamblers, recalling that they'd been dragged out of Dirty Dan's Saloon, one of the roughest in Goldstrike. When he entered the place all conversation stopped, and it took him a moment or two to get his eyes accustomed to the poor light. The smell of the old sawdust-covered floor, vomit, and smoke was strong, and he could see that the bar itself was nothing more than a broad, sanded plank resting on several large beer barrels. Dirty Dan's Saloon was dirty and so were its customers, most of whom appeared to be hard-luck miners or teamsters. There were the usual two or three painted women, and a pair of back doors leading to rooms that would be just as filthy as the saloon itself. In those cribs a customer could wallow in lusty womanhood for a dollar or two.

At the rear of the saloon were the gaming tables, although it was too dark and smoky to see if the pair of cardsharps who had been beaten and jailed were dealing cards.

Longarm moved over to the bar and ordered a whiskey, and the bartender, a large man with a face full of black whiskers, said, "We don't cotton much to lawmen in here, Marshal Long. But since you're just visitin' town and your friend was shot dead, I'll make an exception in your case.''

"Thanks," Longarm replied without much warmth.

When the beer arrived it was bitter, but it only cost a nickel. Longarm lit a cigar and smoked for several minutes until the curious and unfriendly patrons returned to their own conversations.

"I got a question for you," he said to the glowering bartender.

"I got no answers for the law. None."

Longarm motioned the bartender to come closer and said, "I understand that Tilson and Crockett were taking a toll on your girls and gamblers."

"Who said that?"

"I just heard."

"You're a lawman," the bartender stated, wiping his nose on his sleeve. "You ain't gonna want to believe that your friend was dishonest."

"I'm a big boy," Longarm told him. "I can stand up to the truth. Besides, even preachers sometimes go far astray."

"Well," the bartender said, relaxing, "I'm Dirty Dan, and I damn sure didn't appreciate Crockett and Tilson taking a cut off my workers or orderin' 'em to leave town. I warned Crockett that he was playin' a dangerous game."

"Did you threaten Wade?"

"I'm a hell of a lot smarter than that! Crockett could be a real tough sonofabitch, and so can Deputy Tilson. I wasn't afraid of 'em and they wasn't askin' for money from me, so I didn't want no flight. But my gamblers and girls, well, they were real upset."

"Maybe one of them killed Marshal Crockett."

"Maybe," Dan said in a guarded tone. "It would have served the man right. But I'd have shot Deputy Tilson first because he was so damned mean. He almost killed Rudy and Bryce when they got stubborn and refused to pay at first."

"Are they the pair working your back tables?"

"That's right. Tilson beat the hell outta them here, then he did it again after he had 'em in jail." Dan shook his head. "Your friend Marshal Crockett didn't do a damn thing to stop it 'cause he was part of the deal."

Longarm shook his head. "I feel awful bad because Wade was always a good and honest lawman. He just lost sight of things, and started to worry too much about supporting a growing family."

"Yeah," Dan said, obviously not moved by this explanation, "well, we all got problems, don't we? I work eighty hours a week here, and every night I have to break up at least one fight. I been cut, stabbed, shot, and had bottles and chairs busted over my skull, and I sure would like to sit back in a marshal's office and collect dirty money off of someone else for a change."

"I want to talk to Rudy and Bryce."

Dan shook his head. "They're busy."

"What time do they quit?"

"Their shift ends at eight. Rudy and Bryce can't handle the rougher night crowd, and so I pull 'em out of here and send 'em home. They come back about noon and work straight through."

"I'll catch them later then," Longarm said. "Mind if I talk to one of your girls?"

"Mister, if you want their time you got to pay them their money."

"How much for ten minutes?"

"Three dollars and you can ask questions while you hump 'em for all they'll care."

"Fine," Longarm said. "Which girl was maddest about being charged by Crockett and Tilson?"

"They were all madder'n wet wildcats," Dan said. "But I guess Lucy was the worst. She's the skinny one givin' you the evil eye."

"Who do I pay?"

"You pay her three dollars, she pays me one. That's the way it works all over Goldstrike and every other damn mining town I've seen."

Longarm didn't bother finishing his beer, but went over to the woman. She had long black hair, high cheekbones, and a bad complexion scarred by pimples. Lucy also had the eyes of a ferret: cold, merciless, and calculating.

"What the hell are *you* doin' in here?" she demanded. "You come to take your old dead friend's cut off me?"

Longarm shook his head.

"Then what?"

"I come for what I need."

Lucy cackled. "You come for *that*?"

"I'm a man."

"A man who is humpin' Gazella West most afternoons up at the fishing hole."

Longarm chuckled. "Maybe I enjoy variety."

"Fine," Lucy snapped. "It'll cost you three dollars and you can do most anything to me that you want except get really rough."

Longarm extracted the three dollars and gave it to the prostitute. He heard a loud chorus of snickers as he followed Lucy into one of the back rooms. It held a narrow bed covered with an old Army blanket, a nightstand, a dented metal washbasin, soap, towels, and a bottle of whiskey without glasses.

"Big man, if you want to drink whiskey while you do me it will cost you another dollar."

"I just want to talk," Longarm said, closing the door and then leaning against it so that Lucy couldn't get angry and leave before he learned what he wanted to know about the shakedown.

"Talk about what?"

"Marshal Crockett and Deputy Tilson."

"I'd rather screw than talk about them two blood-suckin' bastards."

"How much did they demand from you and the other women in Goldstrike?"

"Five dollars every week. It didn't matter how much business you did, it was the same for everyone."

"And the gamblers?"

"You ain't payin' me enough to tell you everything."

Longarm gave her five more dollars. "Lucy, I'm just trying to find out what happened."

"Them sonsabitches just started shakin' us all down! Me and some of the other girls figured out they were going to rake in at least a hundred dollars a week off us, and probably half that again off the gamblers."

"What if you wouldn't pay?"

"They'd beat the piss outta us, that's what they'd do. And it wasn't just the deputy either. He was the worst, but Crockett would back him up when he did it, and you just knew he'd kill you if you put up much of a fight."

"So you paid for how long?"

Lucy sighed. "It got started the first of this month. Up until then, I thought they were both honest lawmen. But one fine day, they just marched around town and laid down this new law."

"Why didn't anyone tell the mayor or town council?"

Lucy shrugged. "I figured they were all getting a cut."

"I see."

"Gazella says you're hung like a horse," Lucy said, eyes dropping to Longarm's crotch. "As long as you paid, you might as well have your pleasure on me."

"I'm . . . well, I'm just trying to find out who killed my friend," Longarm said awkwardly. "Wade and I went back a long way, and he never did anything like this before. He was a good man."

"He was going rotten! Maybe he was a little better than Tilson, but he'd soon have been just like him. Did you know he even stole Rudy's brand-new boots?"

"No."

"Well, he did. Tilson took 'em but he couldn't get his feet in 'em, so damned if Crockett didn't take 'em instead. I heard the marshal was buried in Rudy's stolen boots, and I hope he walks straight down to Hell in em!"

"Who do you think might have killed him?"

"Could have been anyone that he was takin' protection money off of. Could have been his deputy or Iverson or anyone else. I don't know and I don't care. I just wish someone would kill Tilson too. Is he really the new marshal?"

"I'm afraid so."

"Shit!"

Longarm turned to leave, but then changed his mind. "Lucy, if you hear anyone bragging about killing my friend, I want to know."

"You payin' how much?"

"The reward is two hundred dollars and going up to three hundred. With that much cash, you could leave Goldstrike and start a new line of work."

"Doin' what? Crocheting doilies?" Lucy's laughter was as cold and hard as her feral black eyes.

"Three hundred dollars is a lot of money, but I will require proof and you'll have to testify in a courtroom."

"If I did that, I might not live to spend your damned reward money."

"You would if you took it and ran," Longarm said as he left.

Dirty Dan was standing just outside the crib door, arms folded across his chest. The room was quiet and filled with tension. "Well, lawman?"

Custis's reply was loud enough for everyone in the saloon to hear. "I'll tell you all what I just told Lucy. I'm raising the reward for hard evidence that will hang or send to prison Marshal Wade Crockett's murderer. Starting tomorrow, the reward is going up to three hundred dollars, but don't anyone try to fool me or I'll bust their jaw."

No one said a word, and Longarm headed outside needing some fresh air in his lungs. As he pushed through the front doors, he heard an excited buzz of conversation, and wondered if he was about to learn the identity of Wade's killer. Maybe because it was pretty obvious that anyone in Dirty Dan's would sell their own mother out for that much cash.

"Marshal Long!"

He turned to see a barefoot boy come racing up the boardwalk. The kid came to a sliding stop, and it took him a moment to gather his breath and stammer, "Mrs. Crockett is havin' her baby and Dottie needs you to come right away!"

Now Longarm was running up the street. Gazella stepped out of her little shop and tried to intercept him, but Longarm knocked her flying and kept running. He did not stop until he'd bounded up Rebecca's front stairs and burst into the parlor, where Dottie was leaning over the pregnant woman.

"What can I do!" he gasped.

"Check that water I'm heating on the stove and get some towels out of the cabinets! Then go outside and leave us alone until I need something else."

"That's it?"

"Dammit, what else could a man like you do!" Dottie snapped.

Longarm was offended, but when Rebecca cried out and he saw her legs raise and bend at the knees, he forgot everything except the hot water. "Hang on!"

Rebecca cried out in reply, and Longarm dashed over to the stove and stuck his hand in the kettle.

"Ouch! Dammit, Dottie, it's way, way too hot!"

"Then add cold water. When it's right, pour it into a bowl and bring towels. Hurry!"

Longarm did as he was ordered, and then he was told to go out on the porch. He paced up and down for more than an hour hearing Rebecca's screams, and then . . . then he heard the squall of a newborn babe.

"Rebecca," he shouted, tearing open the front door. "Are you all right!"

"Sure she is, and so is her daughter."

"It's a girl?"

"Daughters usually are," Dottie yelled back at him. "Now go smoke a cigar or something. But don't you come in here until I say so."

"Yes, ma'am!"

Longarm smiled and lit a cigar. He slumped down in a rocking chair and smoked, feeling better than he had since Wade's death. *A daughter, for crying out loud. And Wade had expected his firstborn to be a son. Oh, well,*

*a girl will be more comfort to Rebecca as she is growing
old. Daughters almost always are.*

Longarm didn't have much to do the rest of the evening, and maybe he should have gone to interview Bryce
and Rudy when they ended their shift at Dirty Dan's,
but he wanted to stay close to the house.

"Custis?"

Rebecca's voice sounded so weak he hardly recognized it.

The baby had big blue eyes and soft, pale brown hair.
In truth, Longarm thought all babies were kind of ugly,
but this one was an exception as it owlishly stared up at
him.

"I'm going to name her Faith," Rebecca announced,
looking better than she had since her husband's death.
"I'm going to name her that so that I'll daily be reminded that faith can overcome any hardship. That if I
just have faith in tomorrow and do the best I can for this
child, I'll be fine."

"I think that is a wonderful name," he said, meaning
it as he looked to Dottie for her reaction.

"Dottie was the one to suggest the name," Rebecca
said. "I don't know what I'd have done without her . . .
and you."

"We're both happy to be here," Longarm told her.

"Dottie, why don't you go outside and relax in my
rocking chair and visit with Custis," Rebecca said. "Me
and Faith will be fine."

"Are you sure?"

"Yes, very sure."

"All right."

"And there's some brandy in the cupboard, in case
you two want a little celebration," Rebecca added.

"I'll have some," Longarm said, looking closely at Dottie.

"So will I."

That evening, while Rebecca rested and held and fed Faith, Longarm and Dottie rocked on the front porch and saw two shooting stars.

"When I was growing up in Utah, we always believed that they meant you'd have good luck," Dottie told him.

"I've always heard the same," Longarm said, reaching out and taking her hand.

Dottie did not pull away, but instead smiled. "Custis, I'm happier right now than I've been in a long, long time."

"I'm glad to hear that."

"Why don't you stay and take Wade's place."

He blinked with surprise. "You mean with Rebecca?"

"Sure! She loves you. I can see it in her eyes. And Faith will need a father."

Longarm's laughter was nervous. "I'm not ready for fatherhood and marriage all at the same time."

"Too bad. You'll never find a better woman or a more beautiful baby."

"I guess not, but I'd sort of like to pick my own wife."

"And what kind would you pick that could be nicer than Rebecca?"

"I don't know," he admitted. "Maybe we should all go back to Denver together when Rebecca and the baby are strong enough to travel."

"I'd like that, but I'm not sure that Rebecca will leave."

"We'll just have to talk her into it," Longarm said, content to hold Dottie's hand and watch for another shooting star as the night deepened toward another brand-new day.

Chapter 10

Just as Longarm had ordered, Irwin Duggan had gotten a clean hotel room, a new set of stiff working duds, and a good steak dinner before he'd spent all the rest of his money on whiskey. He'd tried to hold off drinking as long as possible, and had even paid for two nights in a hotel, but he'd forgotten which hotel, and now found himself behind the local livery lying in a pile of not-so-fresh straw.

His mind was preoccupied with how he was going to find out who really murdered Wade Crockett so that he could earn that three hundred dollars in reward money. Duggan was sure that if he ever got that far ahead again, he would swear off drinking for certain, buy a little house, and turn into a solid citizen. Maybe he'd even get himself a wife and go to church, by jingo!

So who could have killed Marshal Crockett? In truth, Duggan knew that it could be any one of several dozen gamblers, and even one of the whores that hated having to pay for the right to earn their tough living.

After getting some cash from the tall federal marshal, Duggan had tried to be sly for a day or two, until the liquor had gotten hold of his reason and he'd started asking folks plain out who might have killed Marshal Crockett. He must have asked a hundred people, but they'd all either just laughed or ordered him away. One gal, though, an ugly one named Norma that worked at the Bonanza Tavern, now *she* had seemed to know the murderer. Or at least, she'd acted like it until the last few precious dollars of Duggan's money was gone. After that, she'd sent him packing in one hell of a hurry.

So here he was, drunk and sleeping in the straw behind Buck Beller's livery again. In the morning, Buck would roust Duggan awake, slap the straw off him, and then put a pitchfork in his hand and say, "It's time to earn your next meal and another night in my straw pile. Get to work cleaning out my stalls."

Duggan didn't mind that work unless he was real sick. Most of the stall-kept horses were high-class animals, and he liked to stroke their coats and tidy up their stalls. If they crapped before he was done, he told 'em that it was all right, and he cleaned up the fresh stuff and put down new straw. There was something good about cleaning up around horses, and he even curried them when he needed a little extra change. Buck was good about helping him out every day so long as Duggan didn't smoke in the barn or get too sick.

All that was well and good, but it didn't change the fact that he was back sleeping in the straw again, broke and cold. Duggan wished he'd bought a heavy woolen coat, but that would have cost way too much money. The other thing that was troublesome was that he had actually paid for this night's lodging in a hotel room . . . somewhere.

"I sure wish I could—hic—remember where I got another room comin'," he muttered drunkenly as he gazed up at the moon and tried to go to sleep. "Sure wish I could."

"How about I help you remember," a soft, almost solicitous voice asked in the darkness.

Duggan thought it was Buck, so he said, "Ain't no use, Mr. Beller. I plumb forgot."

"I didn't. Your paid-up room is at the Sentinel Hotel."

Duggan giggled. "By gawd, you're right, Mr. . . . say, who are you?"

The shadowy figure raised a singletree and then brought it crashing down into Duggan's face, breaking first his nose, then his skull, and then scrambling his whiskey-soaked brains.

"My, my," the shadow man said, "I don't think you are going to be able to get into the Sentinel looking this bad. Guess I'll have to bury you in this pile of straw."

The pile was large and the killer very methodical as he used a pitchfork to dig a long narrow tunnel. He pushed and shoved until Duggan's body was far back under the pile, and then he covered it up and scattered straw over anywhere where there might be blood.

"Too bad you got so curious, Irwin," the murderer remarked with a sad smile. "You should have just stayed a dirty drunk."

Longarm located the two gamblers the next morning, and interviewed both with his usual thoroughness. But neither man wanted to talk, and it was all he could do to get them to admit that, yes, they had been badly beaten by Tilson while Wade Crockett had stood by watching with silent approval.

Rudy was a dark-complexioned man in his mid-fifties with delicate features and walnut-brown eyes that seemed altogether too large for his narrow face. He was the more willing of the two to speak out about the injustice that had been brought about by Goldstrike's lawmen.

"I know you people are underpaid," he grudgingly allowed, "but you took an oath of office and you knew the deal."

"I'm not making excuses," Longarm said.

"Oh? Well, it's no secret that you and them were good friends."

"I was friends with Wade, not Henry Tilson."

"What is the difference? They were both taking our money and knocking hell out of us when we tried to stand up to them. I thought Tilson was going to kill me."

"I'm sorry," Longarm said. "I'm going to put a stop to this illegal extortion."

"Then arrest Marshal Tilson before he really kills someone who won't pay!"

"I can't."

"Why not?"

"Before I do that, I need to find out if he killed Wade."

The man's jaw muscles corded, and he softly patted his side. "I got three broken ribs under this silk vest. I threw up blood for four days after that beating. Have you talked to my friend Bryce?"

"Yes."

"Did he tell you he's having trouble seeing his cards? Bryce now has double vision! Marshal, how long do you think he can make a living at the table with double vision?"

"Not long."

"You're damned right!" Rudy shook his head. "I'm

Portuguese. We're a tough people, but you can't fight the law. We didn't have a chance.''

"But you fought anyway," Longarm reminded the angry gambler.

"Sure, and look what we got. Double vision, broken ribs, and we're payin' anyway."

"I'll stop this and arrest Tilson, but not until I catch my friend's murderer," Longarm repeated.

"That don't help us now."

"I'm sorry. If Tilson killed Wade, I want him to swing for murder. However, if I arrest him now on the charge of extorting money from you people, he'd get off with nothing more than a short prison sentence. That's not nearly enough."

"Listen, I think Tilson is your man. He'd want all of the blood money they were collecting. Who else would stand to gain more by Marshal Crockett's death?"

"You just said that there were a lot of people that would have liked to kill either Wade or Tilson."

"Sure, but . . ."

"It's that 'but' part that a judge would have to consider, and there's no doubt that he'd rule insufficient evidence for a murder trial."

"All right. Then what happens? We just keep getting shaken down until you get your evidence or someone kills Tilson?"

"I'm afraid so."

"Easy for you to hold off," Rudy said. "You're not the one that is getting held up."

"When is your next payment?"

Rudy laughed bitterly. "Tilson and Crockett said they'd collect twice a month, on the first and the fifteenth, just like a couple of damned landlords."

Longarm thought for a moment and then said, "Today

is the tenth. I expect to have my evidence by the fifteenth, certainly by the first of next month. You can stand it that long, can't you?''

"Mister, in Goldstrike, everything costs twice what it would in Denver and it's hard getting ahead here. But I can wait that long and I'll pass the word to—''

"No,'' Longarm said. "I don't want Tilson to know my game. Just keep this under your hat.''

"What hat?''

"Then up your sleeve,'' Longarm said with a tight smile. "Let's give Marshal Tilson enough rope to hang himself.''

"Sounds good.''

"Do you think that Delbert Iverson or his father had anything to do with my friend's murder?''

"Delbert could have done it. He was mean and dumb enough.''

"The only one that will know for sure is his father, and I can't hold him in jail any longer without proof.''

Rudy shook his head. "Sounds like you're just waiting for something to happen.''

"And it will,'' Longarm vowed. "Three hundred dollars is enough money to overcome fear. Someone in this town knows who the killer is, and he's going to come for my money.''

"And what if he already has a bundle of money and would prefer to keep on living?''

Longarm didn't have an answer for that, so he simply shrugged his broad shoulders and let Rudy know that their conversation was over.

Buck Beller had grown up in Oregon and been a sailor, but finally got tired of the Pacific Ocean fog and rough, cold weather. Adventurous and fun-loving, he'd migrated east to Colorado and had become a first-rate cowboy. Now well past his prime, and a little stove up in the joints from his years of cold ocean fishing and breaking outlaw broncs that no one else would dare to tame, he was more than content to care for saddle horses. He liked them far better than people, better than dogs, and almost as much as stray cats, which were found in great abundance in his barn and around his dusty livery lot. Occasionally, though, the cats got stomped on by a horse, and then Buck was devastated for days. But he never blamed a horse because cats could be pesky and it was just their nature to get underfoot.

Cats of all ages, colors, and sizes followed Buck throughout his daily work routine. He had eight permanent boarders in the barn, and a constant turnover of new horses that were generally kept in outdoor stalls or in one of several corrals. But Buck insisted that the corralled horses were friendly to other horses and not likely to cripple each other with hooves or teeth.

This was the second morning that he had not seen Duggan, and Buck was a bit miffed because he was stiff in all his aching joints and needed help. To his thinking, if Duggan was going to quit on him or become unreliable, then he'd have to hire part-time help to clean all the indoor stalls and take on some of the general work around the place.

So Buck spent this morning going from stall to stall and cleaning. Unlike Duggan, whom he did not completely trust, Buck removed the expensive horses from their stalls one by one so that he could do a better cleaning. But that was slow, and it was nearly noon before he finished the last one. Then, with cats in tow, Buck went outside to pitch yet another load of straw into the wheelbarrow so that it would be ready in the morning.

It was the calico cat that kept fussing and mewing whenever Buck had gotten a fresh load of straw. And now she was practically having fits, hissing and carrying on with all the hairs of her tail standing out as stiff as those on a bottle brush. Buck was trying to figure out what her problem was when he saw the bottom of a badly worn shoe. The calico had sniffed and even scratched the straw away just enough to make this discovery visible.

Buck gulped. He instinctively knew that he was looking at Duggan's foot and that the man was dead. Otherwise, Duggan would have been snoring. Duggan was a helluva snorer, and Buck figured the only reason he would be back inside that straw pile and so quiet was that he had to be dead.

"Easy," Buck said to the other cats gathered around and now joining the calico in hissing. "I'll get our friend out of there. Just get back."

He grabbed Duggan by the ankle and started dragging him out, and that was bad enough, but when Buck got to where he could see the poor man's disfigured and blood-covered face, he turned and vomited. It took him nearly half an hour before he could stand and breathe properly, and then he had to fight to go back and stare with morbid fascination at the body.

"Holy cow," he whispered to his nervous, hissing cats, "this is a murder!"

For a moment, Buck thought he was in deep trouble because someone might accuse *him* of murder. But then he calmed down some more and looked around. Sure enough, he saw the blood-caked singletree lying inside the straw tunnel up where what was left of Duggan had rested.

"What am I going to do now!" he moaned out loud.

Buck hated Marshal Tilson with an abiding passion. He'd heard a lot of stories about the man's sadistic treatment of the weak, the drunk, and those who had fallen on especially hard times. Tilson was mean and he was dangerous. Yet he was now the only law in Goldstrike. So what else was there to do but to find him and then bring him here to see the body?

Buck couldn't think of a single alternative, so he started for the marshal's office, but then he just happened to spot that big federal marshal who was offering a three-hundred-dollar reward for the name of whoever had murdered his friend.

Buck decided that the man who might have murdered Crockett might also have murdered poor Irwin Duggan, although there seemed to be no real connection.

"Marshal?" he called, hurrying over to Longarm.

"Yeah?"

"I got something I have to show you," Buck whispered, hoping like hell that Tilson didn't just happen to be watching. "There's a man been murdered in my livery straw pile."

"Murdered?"

"Head bashed in with a singletree."

"Why don't you tell Marshal Tilson?"

"Because I don't like him at all," Buck answered. "So I'll let you see it first, in case the same man that murdered Marshal Crockett also murdered my friend."

"Let's take a look," Longarm decided, knowing it was out of his legal boundaries to investigate, but the hell with it.

When he saw Duggan's body, Longarm knew that the murders were connected. Duggan had been asking too many questions, and when he'd gotten into his cups, he must have asked the real murderer the wrong question, sealing his sad fate.

"You see anybody here that might have killed Duggan?"

"No, sir! How long has he been dead?"

"He was probably killed night before last. No barking of your dogs or anything at all?"

"I have cats, not dogs, and they don't bark, and I never heard anything or seen anything until the calico cat, the one I call Buttermilk, she got crazy here and showed me what was wrong."

Longarm studied the ground, and it was plenty soft enough to have lots of tracks showing. "I suppose that you have tromped around here a lot, huh?"

"Sure!"

"Take off your boot," Longarm ordered, removing one of Duggan's as well.

"What are you gonna do with 'em?"

Longarm could see that Buck and Duggan wore about the same size boot. "I'm going over this ground with a fine-tooth comb, hoping to find either a bigger or smaller print. Anyone else have a reason to come to this exact spot?"

"No. I'm the only one that gets straw to clean the stalls each morning . . . or maybe I should say he and I were. Now, I guess I better find another man."

"Give me an hour and then go find and tell Marshal Tilson."

"I'd sure rather you did it. I hate that low-down bastard."

"I'd do it, but I need to keep this investigation just between ourselves," Longarm said. "Okay?"

"All right. You think that he's gonna charge me with murder?"

114

"No," Longarm said. "I don't."

"Well, he might! He wants to stay on as town marshal, and he's going to need someone to make the scapegoat so he can look good."

Longarm realized the man's fears were not without some basis, so he said, "Do you sleep with anyone at night?"

"Just cats."

"I'll do what I can to make sure you aren't jailed."

"Damn!" Buck fussed. "I got a lot of animals here that need me. If I was to get tossed in jail even for a day or two, who'd take care of 'em all!"

"I would," Longarm said. "But it won't happen."

"I sure hope not," Buck fretted. "I—I maybe should have gone straight to Tilson, but—"

"No," Longarm interrupted. "You did exactly the right thing. I know you didn't kill Duggan. You were about his only friend, weren't you?"

"Just me and the cats. They liked him plenty too. He had a good heart under what he showed on the outside. Duggan was real proud of how you asked him to help, and he took that duty seriously. I don't think he'll even get buried proper, because he didn't have no money and I ain't got much either."

"I'll see that he gets a good burial," Longarm promised out of a strong sense of responsibility. "I'll see to that."

"If I wasn't so broke all the time, then I'd . . ."

Longarm placed a hand on Buck Beller's shoulder. He could see the dust trails of tears that the older man had already shed over his friend.

"It's all right," Longarm said. "I'll take care of the funeral expenses and I'll handle Tilson."

Buck dipped his pointy chin. "Duggan said you were

a good lawman, not like Crockett and Tilson."

Longarm felt a stab of pain to hear that his best friend was seen in the same bad light as Henry Tilson, but he didn't say anything more as he examined the murder weapon and then the body, before getting down on his hands and knees and starting to study each and every footprint near the pile of straw.

"I guess I'll go get Marshal Tilson now, huh?" the liveryman finally said.

"Give me ten more minutes."

"You've already been down there for nearly an hour."

"I know, but I've found some tracks that are much larger than yours and Duggan's. I just want to make sure that they are all the same size and made by one man."

"You think that they are the killer's?" Buck asked with sudden interest.

"They might be."

"Holy cow!"

"Holy cats," Longarm replied, brushing three or four of the curious creatures out of his way. They were a real bother, but he, like poor Duggan and this liveryman, liked cats a lot.

"All right," he said finally. "Go get Tilson."

"You going to be here when he comes?"

"No," Longarm answered, "but don't worry. I'll just conveniently come by a few minutes later."

"Don't be late now!" Buck said, looking scared. "That big sonofabitch just might try to beat a confession out of me."

"I won't give him the chance. I'll tell you what. I'll be waiting just inside your barn. If he so much as yells at you, I'll be out here in a second."

"Good enough," Buck said, looking extremely relieved as he limped away.

Longarm took his final measurements, then penciled a copy of the large boot print on a sheet of paper and shoved it deep into his coat pocket. For his money, he was betting it would match that of Marshal Henry Tilson.

Chapter 11

Buck was plenty scared as he stood outside the marshal's office. Many years ago as a wild boy, he'd been savagely beaten by an Oregon lawman, and still carried the inner as well as the outer scars. From that day to this he'd tried his damnedest to stay clear of lawmen and walk the straight and narrow road as an honest, hardworking citizen. Buck didn't drink or smoke and he never gambled. He just worked and wondered if he'd ever find a girl to match the sweetheart he'd loved so dearly back in Oregon.

Shall I knock on his door first or just go in? he asked himself. *They say that good people like me pay lawmen's wages with taxes, but I don't think that would mean much to a fella like Henry Tilson. Don't want to make him any more upset than he already will be when I tell him about poor Duggan getting his face and skull broken.*

Buck knocked, and Tilson shouted, "Gawdammit, the door is unlocked, so open it!"

"Yes, sir," Buck replied, pushing inside, removing his hat, and pressing it to his chest.

"What the hell do *you* want?" Tilson demanded.

"I . . . I, well, I . . ."

"For chrissakes, spit it out, you old half-wit!"

"It's Irwin. He's dead."

"Who?"

"Irwin Duggan. You arrested him a bunch of times for being drunk, and I found his body hidden in the straw pile behind my barn."

Tilson dropped his feet down from his desktop with a thud. "You sure?"

"Yes, sir! Buttermilk found him."

"Who is Buttermilk?" Tilson demanded, coming to his feet and hitching up his gun belt.

"She's my calico cat."

"A *cat* found the body?"

"Yes, sir!"

"Let's go take a look."

"It . . . it ain't pretty, Marshal."

"Duggan was ugly alive—he can't be much worse-looking dead."

Buck didn't agree, but he didn't argue either. Instead, he backed out of the marshal's office, shoved his hat back down on his balding head, and took off fast for his livery. He didn't slow down until he was standing beside the body and looking at the barn where Longarm was hiding.

"You still there, ain't ya?"

"Shhhh! Stop looking at me."

"He's mad."

"I don't care. I won't let him hurt you. Now pretend you're alone."

Buck tried to pretend, but his heart was racing. When the marshal came around the side of the barn and saw the body, he pulled up short and stared, then slowly came forward.

120

"That's Duggan, all right. You know who killed him?"

"No, sir!"

"Maybe you did, huh?"

Buck paled, and got so excited he could hardly speak. "Oh, no, sir!"

"If you can't tell me who did it, I'm going to have to arrest you as the most likely suspect," Tilson said, advancing on the liveryman. "That's the law."

Longarm had heard enough. "The hell it's the law," he said, coming out of the barn. "You got no evidence at all that this man killed Duggan. In fact, only an idiot would suggest that a man would murder someone and hide his body on his own premises."

"Who the hell do you think you are, telling me how to do my job!" Tilson's hand dropped close to the six-gun at his side. "Maybe *you* killed this man!"

"I was thinking the same thing about you," Longarm replied. "And if you're thinking about reaching for your Colt, you'd better think again because I'll shoot you down."

"Maybe, and maybe not."

For a moment, Longarm was sure that Tilson was going to draw. Wade had said that his deputy was extremely fast and accurate with a gun, and Tilson seemed crazy enough to take the chance. But then a couple of men who boarded horses with Buck came around the corner looking for him, and the distraction averted the gunfight.

"What's going on here?" one of the men asked before his eyes fell on the body.

"Oh, my gawd!" his friend cried. "Who was *that*!"

"Old Irwin Duggan," Buck said. "You men know anybody who wanted him dead?"

121

"Hell, no!" One looked at the other, and then they both wheeled around and disappeared.

"Well?" Longarm said. "You going to go find this man's killer, or what?"

Tilson cursed and departed, yelling over his shoulder, "Neither one of you better leave Goldstrike."

"Now why would I do that?" Buck asked.

"He's just sounding off trying to save face," Longarm answered.

"You think he will try to arrest me?"

"Nope." Longarm went over to the boot prints just made by Tilson, and pulled the pattern he'd drawn earlier from his pocket. He laid the pattern down over the fresh print, then frowned and stood up again.

"They match?" Buck asked expectantly.

"Nope."

"Well, then, who?"

"I have no idea," Longarm said bitterly a moment before he walked away shaking his head.

That evening, Longarm got a little drunk on Rebecca's front porch. He was so damned frustrated that he couldn't see straight, and completely baffled as to who had ambushed Wade and then murdered poor Irwin Duggan.

Dottie came out to see if she could cheer him up. "Whoever killed them doesn't have to be the same person, does it?"

"No," Longarm admitted. "I've been thinking that it was Tilson, but I guess I was wrong."

"Maybe only *half* wrong," Dottie said. "Tilson is still the best suspect for murdering Mr. Crockett, but maybe he has accomplices and one of *them* murdered poor Mr. Duggan."

122

"That's entirely possible, but I've got no evidence as to either killer! No evidence at all."

"Something will turn up," Dottie promised. "Someone will come to earn that reward."

Longarm had purchased a fresh bottle of brandy, and he offered Dottie some in his glass. She drank and cleared her throat, then had a little more.

"I never saw a Mormon woman drink like you."

"Maybe I'm not a Mormon woman."

Longarm sighed. "Dottie, I'm just worn plumb out trying to figure who killed Wade, and whether they were trying to kill me on this porch and got him by mistake. And then whether poor Duggan was murdered because he was asking too many questions."

"What are you trying to say to me?"

"Just that I don't have the mental energy to try and figure out *your* mysterious past. How you got to Goldstrike and where you came from and why you're staying."

"I'm staying because Rebecca and her baby need me and I've never been needed before. Is that clear enough?"

Longarm retrieved his glass, drained it, and refilled it in brooding silence.

"Are you going to get blotted?"

"Get what?" ·

"Blotted."

"You must mean sotted. And yes, I just might."

"That sure won't help you figure out who the murderers are."

"Tilson turned Iverson free. I couldn't do a thing about it."

"I don't think he killed either man, so what does it matter."

"Maybe he knows who did," Longarm mused.

"Maybe, but I doubt it."

"Why?"

"He had no friends," Dottie said. "Just customers. There's a big difference."

"I suppose so. Is the man as dangerous as his son?"

Dottie took another big drink, smacked her pretty lips, and said, "I suppose that he might be."

"Thanks, that helps a lot," Longarm said.

"You're really down, aren't you?" Dottie said, coming out of her rocker and kneeling at his knees.

"I am," he admitted. "How long has Wade been dead now? Two weeks."

"Ten days."

"Well, in ten days I've found out absolutely nothing. I'm no closer to solving a case I've sworn to solve than I was the night he was murdered. And to top that, I am probably responsible for Duggan getting his skull crushed."

"You take a lot of responsibility on, don't you."

"What is that supposed to mean?"

"It means that you have two murders to solve and then you want to take care of Rebecca and me. What else? I can see that your shoulders are very broad, but you can't do everything."

Longarm had to smile. "So far, I haven't solved anything. Not one damned thing."

Dottie took his drink from his fist and placed it on the porch before she sat down on his lap, wrapped her arms around his neck, and said, "I think you need something better than brandy tonight to distract your poor mind."

"Oh?"

She slipped her fingers between the buttons of his shirt and whispered, "I think you need *me*."

Longarm blinked. "Do you know what you are saying, or has the brandy already gone to your brain?"

"I'm not at all the innocent little Mormon girl you think I am."

"Keep talking."

Dottie kissed his mouth. "Rebecca is napping and so is Faith. I don't have time to explain, and anyway, there is something else I'd rather do with you right now."

Longarm got the message in a hurry, and it wasn't but a few moments later that they were undressed and lying in his bedroll on the front porch.

"You're so small I'm afraid that I might hurt you," he whispered as he sucked greedily on her beautiful breasts and stroked her silken thighs.

"I'm big enough," she panted, guiding his throbbing manhood into herself and then moaning with pleasure.

"Yeah," he said, "I can see you're right."

"No more talk. Just action."

"You got it," he said, hips beginning to move in slow circles as he stroked her into a matching movement that was nothing short of ecstasy for them both.

He rode her for a long time, and then she bit his ear and whispered that it was time she was on top. Longarm understood, and he rolled over, staring up at her beautiful face, now glistening with perspiration, and admiring her long, shiny black hair.

She knelt on him and began to move up and down, mouth open, tongue flicking, breasts heaving. Longarm was on fire, and his fingers dug into her lean hips and guided her buttocks in her increasingly frenzied movement.

"Where have you been all my life?" she moaned, head and hair dropping as she stared down at him with eyes glazed with passion. "I've never had a man like you."

"No more talk," he teased. "Remember?"

In reply, she fell forward and kissed his mouth, her tongue probing even as his rod was pistoning in and out of her slick honey pot. And that was the way they came together, crying out in the night, his heels beating on the porch floor, exchanging wet and wild kisses as if there would never be any more.

"Damn, Dottie," he grunted when she finally climbed off him and began to pull on her dress, now fearful of Rebecca suddenly appearing. "I sure had you pegged wrong!"

"Do you think less of me now that you know I'm not some frightened little virgin?" Her tone was defensive.

"No, gawd, no!" He reached for her, but she retreated. "What's wrong?"

"Nothing," she said, but he could tell from the tone of her voice that it wasn't true.

Longarm pulled on his pants and shirt, then collapsed back in the rocking chair. "Dottie, I've got to know what you are thinking."

"Why? Men don't care about women's thoughts."

"Stop it! Of course I care. I want you and Rebecca to come to stay with me in Denver until . . ."

"Until what? Until you tire of me or are sent off somewhere again?"

He ignored the sharpness of her words. "Until you decide what you want."

"I'd like *you*," she said. "And poor Rebecca would like her husband back, but wanting doesn't mean a thing in this world."

"Talk to me! Tell me what you mean."

"I mean that there was a time when I believed that

people fell in love and lived happily ever after. That's all.''

"But you don't anymore?''

"Come on!'' she cried. "Do you?''

"No,'' he heard himself answer. "But maybe we could . . .''

He couldn't finish.

"Fall in love and live happily ever after while you go off to arrest and kill outlaws? While I wait in Denver? Thanks for the flattering thought, but no, thanks!''

Longarm reached for the brandy and drank it straight from the bottle. He was more confused than ever now, and decided that he had better get seriously drunk or else go to sleep.

"You're tired and upset and confused,'' Dottie said. "You need to do more resting and fishing.''

"Fishing?''

"Sure. Isn't that what Gazella West wants?''

"To hell with her!'' he snapped.

"Well,'' Dottie said, taking the bottle from his hand and going into the house, "at least get some sleep tonight.''

Longarm heard the baby then. Dottie must have heard her waking up a few moments earlier, and that was why she'd cut their talk short.

Damned confusing, that girl. Longarm lay down on his bedroll, laced his fingers behind his head, and promised that he would not think about murderers all night long. Nope, instead he'd think of the beautiful, passionate Dottie Quigley or whatever her name was, and he'd sleep like a log until morning.

Chapter 12

It was late the next morning when Longarm stirred on the porch. He looked up, blinked, and there was Dottie smiling down at him with a steaming cup of coffee in her hand.

"How do you feel?"

"I don't know yet."

"I hope this will help you wake up and decide."

Longarm sat up and took the coffee. He blew the steam off the rim and studied her beautiful pixie face. "Was I dreaming last night or did we . . ."

"We did," Dottie replied, not blushing or looking the least bit regretful as he'd feared. "And wasn't it wonderful?"

"I sure thought so."

"So did I. Can we do it again tonight, same time and same place?"

"Sure, but—"

"I think," Dottie said, interrupting, "that you should go fishing and forget all that murder business for a day."

"How can I do that with two unsolved murders?"

"Sometimes, when you worry and think too hard on a problem, the solution won't come. However, if you put it out of your mind, and I mean completely, the answer magically appears. Haven't you ever had that happen after a good night's sleep?''

"Yeah, I have," Longarm admitted.

"Then give it a try now. Go fishing and relax. Take a nap by the stream and see what happens."

"I will," he decided. Longarm brightened and tipped his coffee cup to her in a happy salute. "By gosh, that's exactly what I'll do! I just wish you could come with me."

"So do I," Dottie said. "From what I hear, that must be a *very* romantic place where you fish."

Longarm blushed. "You're thinking of Gazella."

"I didn't say that." Dottie smiled innocently at him. "But I have heard the gossip."

"Damn the gossip! I'm through with Gazella, now that we're together."

"I certainly hope so," Dottie replied, kissing his cheek.

Longarm collected his fishing pole and gear, saddened that Wade was not going with him anymore. The truth was that Longarm had never been an avid fisherman. Mostly he enjoyed just the relaxation it offered or the good company of a friend. No matter, he would do as Dottie suggested and simply take a short break and try not to think about murder.

The pines and white-barked aspen were beautiful and offered plenty of cool shade that morning as Longarm hiked up to his usual fishing spot. He removed his boots, gun, and holster, rigged his pole, baited his hook, and cast his line. Nothing happened, but he was content to just settle in for a nap if the fish didn't feel like biting.

He must have dozed off because the tip of his pole was suddenly jumping. The pole damn near got away from him before he could fully awaken and start reeling in what he was sure was a very large trout. Longarm waded out into the bone-numbing water, and he could see the silvery monster.

"Dammit, Wade!" he gleefully shouted across the swift-moving water. "I'd give anything if you could see this granddaddy of Crystal Creek!"

Longarm played the fish carefully, giving line when it made an especially hard run, and then taking more back when the trout rested. At last, he had the fish up near the bank, where it flopped and twisted in the shallows, making it difficult to grab and haul onto the bank.

"Come on," he pleaded, "you will make a dinner tonight!"

But the fish had other ideas. When Longarm tried to hook his forefinger into its gills, the trout jumped, causing him to lose his balance on the mossy rocks underfoot and do a flop of his own. The pole caught in between a pair of submerged boulders, and the frantic fish broke the line and vanished.

"Dammit," Longarm swore.

He heard giggling, and turned to see Gazella standing where he'd left his boots.

"Hey, big boy! Big fish got away, huh!"

"Yeah, it did," Longarm said, shivering and disgusted with his sorry performance. "And now I'm soaked."

"Better undress and dry your clothes on a bush."

The water was ice cold, and Longarm was already covered with gooseflesh. He saw no other alternative than to do as she suggested. Dislodging his fishing pole and then sloshing back to shore, Longarm shucked his sopping-wet clothes and found a handy bush to lay them

131

out upon. When he turned around, he saw that Gazella had also removed her clothes.

"Now wait a minute," he said, taking a step back and raising his hands in self-defense. "Gazella, I need to rest today. That's all I want, a little rest and relaxation!"

"Sure," she said, licking her lips, "that and some hard and fast lovin'."

"Gazella, no!"

"Gonna play tough to get today, huh, big boy! Well, that suits me fine! I like to play games too!"

She lowered her head and charged with outspread arms. Longarm tried to dodge her, but he slipped on the wet grass and Gazella covered him like butter on a hot pancake. And damned if his body didn't betray his will and . . . well, the next thing he knew, they were humping like crazy.

"Oh, struggle a little more," Gazella pleaded. "It makes me even more excited!"

Longarm wasn't going to struggle, but after this was over, he was definitely going to have a serious discussion with Gazella and tell her that he was leaving for Denver and wanted Dottie, not her, to come along.

When Gazella finally gasped, shuddered, and shook like a huge bowl of vanilla pudding, she rolled off him and gasped, "I can't understand why we don't do this about three times a day, Custis."

"Because I'm not up to it."

"Of course you are!" As if to prove her words, Gazella reached down, grabbed his manhood, and began to jack his foreskin up and down like the handle of a water pump. "I'll bet I can get you to stand up tall in no time!"

Longarm pulled her hand away and scrambled out of

her reach. "Gazella, there is something I *have* to tell you."

"Are we leaving for Denver together after all?" she asked with joy radiating across her face.

"No," he began, not wanting to hurt her feelings or get her riled. "But . . ."

A cry of surprise cut Longarm's words short. "Oh, Custis, how could you!"

He twisted around, and there was Dottie holding Wade's fishing pole with eyes already spilling tears. "Damn you, Custis!"

Dottie hurled the fishing pole down, turned, and raced back into the trees for town.

"Aw, shit," Longarm groaned. "Now we've done it."

"Done what?" Gazella asked. "Everyone in Goldstrike knows what has been going on between us up here."

"Yeah, but I'd promised *one* of them that things were going to change."

"That little Mormon bitch!"

"All right, that's it," Longarm exploded, jumping to his feet. "We're finished. No more of this screwing instead of fishing."

"Because of that meatless little strumpet?"

"Gazella, I happen to think of her very differently."

"You've screwed her! Is that why you haven't been coming by lately to see me?"

"That and a couple of murders I'm trying to solve."

"I can't believe that you'd be interested in someone as small as that!" Gazella wailed. "And . . . and don't you know that she already has an old Mormon husband?"

"What?"

133

"That's right. She's married. You're a lawman, for crying out loud! Ain't screwin' someone's wife illegal?"

Longarm groaned. "I should have stayed in town and kept trying to find out who killed Wade and poor Duggan instead of coming up here and getting into all this trouble."

Gazella was on her feet and grabbing her dress. "I've never been so humiliated in my entire life. The fact that you'd want that little Mormon bitch over me is just— just way too much to bear!"

And with that, she tore Longarm's wet clothes off the bush and tossed them far out in the creek.

"Hey!" he cried. "What did you do that for!"

"You can just walk your naked ass back to Goldstrike for all I care!"

Longarm charged into the water, but rocks punished the bottoms of his tender feet. Cussing and fuming, he started back in time to see Gazella snatch up his boots and fling them far over his head into the swift water.

"Dammit!" Longarm shouted. "Dammit anyway!"

Gazella tore his six-gun out of his holster and aimed it at Longarm, who dove headfirst into the creek. When he ran out of air and had to surface, Gazella still had the gun pointed at him. "I ought to shoot your balls off!"

"Look, I'm sorry!"

"Sorry is right!"

"Put the gun down."

"No!"

Longarm had reached his limit. "Put the damned gun down or kill me! But if you fail, I'll kill you!"

Gazella dropped the gun, made an obscene gesture, and stomped off down the trail cursing.

Longarm watched in dismay as his boots merrily

bobbed and danced on the swift current until they rounded a bend and were gone.

This is awful, he thought, sitting down butt-naked on the bank and cradling his head in his hands. *The only way it could get any worse is if everyone in town knew and came up here to have a good laugh.*

"Gazella would do that!" he exclaimed, jumping up and tearing a limb from a bush, then covering himself and tiptoeing painfully down the rocky trail. "Ouch! Ouch!"

It took Longarm nearly two hours to sneak down to the edge of town, and he swore in anger to see a number of laughing townspeople hurrying up the trail to catch him in the height of his humiliation. Obviously, Gazella had told everyone that the federal marshal was stark naked up by the fishing hole, and he'd have bet anything she hadn't bothered to explain why.

Longarm didn't know what to do. The Crockett house was in the middle of Goldstrike. To reach it, he'd have to navigate the boundary streets, and there was no way he could do that without being observed, probably by children as well as a few ladies.

I'm stuck, he thought morosely. *There is no way that I can get to Rebecca's without being seen before dark.*

Muttering imprecations, Longarm hid in the bushes, thinking that this might become one of the very longest and worst days of his entire life.

It was about nine o'clock in the evening when Longarm finally sneaked back onto Rebecca's porch. He wrapped a blanket around himself, and then tried to enter the house and get a spare set of clean clothes. But Rebecca was sitting inside waiting with Baby Faith nursing in her arms.

"Well," she said looking more tired than angry, "now we're down to just the three of us—you, me, and Faith."

"What happened to Dottie?"

"She was devastated," Rebecca replied. "She told me what you did and she was really crying."

"Listen, Rebecca, I feel awful."

"You should!"

"I told Gazella we were finished. That's why she got so mad and tossed my clothes, even my boots, into the creek, and I need to find some clothes."

"They're in that chest on the floor over by the wall. I washed and ironed them."

"Where do you think Dottie went?"

"Back to her husband somewhere in Utah."

"Why?"

"Because she is legally married."

"Not if he's a polygamist!"

"Custis, you have really disappointed me this time," Rebecca said with a shake of her head. "That was a good woman and you broke her heart."

"I'll make things right."

"I think it is far too late for that now."

"I don't. Did she say how she was getting back and exactly where this 'husband' lives?"

"Yes. In a small Mormon community named Pine on the Virgin River in southern Utah."

"I've ridden through there and I'll overtake Dottie long before she arrives. And . . ." Longarm stopped. "Rebecca, what about you and Faith?"

"We can get by for a spell. Just catch that girl and apologize with all your heart, Custis. Tell her that you love her and that it will never happen again."

"Well, Rebecca, hang on now," Longarm said, pulling on a dry shirt. "I'm right taken with Dottie, but I'm a long way from wanting to tie the marriage knot."

Rebecca's temper erupted. "I'd like to tie a knot around your cheatin' neck, Custis! Now you do as I say. Dottie wasn't one to unburden her sorrows or hardships, but she did tell me that she was forced to marry a man who is well into his sixties."

"What?"

"She hated this man, but he has considerable property, wives, and wealth. Now, if she does reach him before you can stop her, she'll be a twice-wronged woman."

"I won't let that happen. I've got a pretty good horse and . . ."

"I believe she bought your horse and saddle."

"Tell me that's not true."

"Oh, but it is. Dottie tossed thirty dollars in gold nuggets on the table. It's for you. She asked me if that was enough compensation. I lied and told her it was, but that you'd rather she not go. She went anyway, but we had a very sad and tearful farewell."

"Rebecca, I'm just damned sorry," Longarm said, buckling on his gun belt. "I messed up something awful this time."

"You sure did."

Longarm grabbed his gear, hoping Buck would sell him a good mount and saddle for just thirty dollars. Since he didn't have extra boots, he had to cut the toes off a pair of Wade's old work boots so that they would accommodate his bigger feet.

"Dammit, Rebecca, this is about the worst vacation I've ever had! I would have been ten times better off staying in Denver or going out in the field on another case."

Rebecca's eyes filled with tears. "I hope you don't really mean that. Because if you hadn't come, then you wouldn't have seen Wade for the last time, nor would you have been here to meet Dottie or help me and Faith."

He hurried over and hugged her tightly. "I *didn't* mean it," he confessed. "It's just that things seemed to have gone from bad to worse in a hell of a big hurry."

"Go find Dottie before she reaches Pine. Say whatever you have to to bring her back to Colorado," Rebecca pleaded. "Dottie is strong, but what she saw today was sort of the last straw, and she's not thinking clearly anymore. She's seen too much sadness for a girl her age, and I think if she rejoins her husband and his family, everything inside of her that is fresh and free will be forever lost."

"I'll do it!" he vowed, scooping up the pouch of gold nuggets that Dottie had left on the table.

Longarm headed off for Buck Beller's stable in his ridiculous work boots and with his bedroll tied up and stuffed under his arm along with his rifle and saddlebags. He ignored the laughter of men who recognized him as he stomped up the main street. But he couldn't ignore the sight of Marshal Henry Tilson, who suddenly stiffened and whose fingers now splayed over the butt of his gun.

"You're under arrest for murder, Long!"

"I'm not going to jail on any crazy charge like that."

Longarm dropped his bedroll and saddlebags. His hand moved across his waist, and he was prepared to use his cross-draw if that was what it took to avoid arrest and save Dottie from an old man in Utah.

Tilson took a deep breath and expelled it slowly. "You're under arrest for the murder of Lucy Peterson."

"Who?"

"The whore you hired and who worked in Dirty Dan's Saloon."

"I didn't 'hire' her! What are you talking about?"

"You hired her, all right, then you stabbed her to death last night in order to keep her from telling everyone the truth."

"Which is?"

"Which is that you murdered Irwin Duggan and stuffed his body in that pile of straw!"

"I don't believe how this day is going."

"Huh?"

"I said, this is *definitely* the worst day of my life."

"And," Tilson added, "it's going to be the last day of your life if you don't raise your hands and surrender."

Longarm didn't want to kill Tilson, and of course there was the very real possibility that *he* might be the one to die. But Dottie was heading for Utah, and there just was no time to work things out while in jail.

"Make your play," Longarm growled.

Tilson was very, very fast. But he must have been afraid down deep inside because, although he got off the first shot, it went wide. Longarm, on the other hand, was a tad slower and considerably more accurate. His bullet struck Tilson and spun him around like a boy's top. The man collapsed in the dirt, thrashing and screaming. Someone yelled over in front of Dirty Dan's Saloon and opened fire on Longarm from the shadows.

Longarm knew that it was too late to reach Buck and negotiate the sale or rental of a good, fast horse. So he picked the tallest and fastest-looking animal tied in front of the closest saloon, and he untied it in a hail of bullets.

He escaped by hanging onto the side of the saddle as the tall horse charged down the street.

"Dammit!" he screamed at the moon as he reined the animal west toward Utah. "This is *definitely* the worst day of my life!"

Chapter 13

As he rode toward Utah the next day, Longarm didn't even want to consider the mess he was now in. He'd wronged Dottie, left behind poor Rebecca and Faith, shot a town marshal, and stolen a horse. It was enough to get a fella down. All he knew for sure was that Henry Tilson wanted to railroad him into being a scapegoat. And knowing how corrupt the town seemed to be, Longarm had little doubt that the judge might go along with Tilson's plan and even get him convicted of murder. That would eliminate a big headache, and probably get Tilson a raise in pay and a permanent job as the marshal of Goldstrike.

Because of that, Longarm reasoned that he'd really had no choice but to make a stand and shoot Tilson. At least he hadn't killed the man—or maybe he should have and just let the cards fall where they might. He could overtake and save Dottie, then get her to Denver and send for Rebecca. Marshal Billy Vail would be furious about all the complications, but he'd help Longarm and see that justice was served. That might even mean sending another federal lawman to investigate the murders of Wade and Duggan.

Longarm couldn't believe how complicated everything had become since he'd arrived. All he really wanted was to catch the murderer of his best friend, and then remove Tilson from office so that he could no longer extort protection money from the prostitutes, gamblers, and whoever else he was milking.

But first, there was this matter of catching Dottie and preventing her from making a huge mistake. And so, as Longarm rode through the day on the tall, fast horse, he looked for tracks and wondered if he was even on Dottie's trail. It seemed likely, for there were very few good roads leading down the western slopes of the Rockies and toward Pine, Utah. Dottie would be so upset she would probably not be thinking about anymore following her, and so would take the most direct route available, which was the one that Longarm was now following.

About sundown, he got a break when a friendly mule skinner hauling lumber from a nearby sawmill answered, "Yeah, I saw that pretty little gal and she was sure sad-looking. I asked if she was in trouble, but she didn't even answer."

"How far ahead is she by now?"

"Not more than two hours. You her husband or something?"

"A friend. What color horse was she riding?"

"Bay gelding. Nice-looking animal." The mule skinner frowned. "Why you askin' so many questions about that gal?"

"Because she's riding my horse."

"She *stole* your horse?"

"Not exactly. She bought it for thirty dollars, but I didn't want to sell because . . . aw, never mind."

"Then whose horse are *you* ridin' now?"

142

"I don't know," Longarm said truthfully. "I stole it."

"You—"

"Mister, I sure appreciate your help but it's complicated."

"Don't you know that horse stealin' is a hangin' offense?"

"Sure, I'm a federal marshal."

The mule skinner rolled his eyes and released the brake to his wagon. He drove off looking completely confused, and Longarm couldn't blame him. Maybe he shouldn't even have tried to explain.

Knowing that Dottie was only a couple of hours up the road gave Longarm's spirits a big boost. He pushed his horse to the limits of its speed and endurance, but the sun was going down fast. Longarm continued riding hard into the fading light, and finally arrived at the small mining town of Jumbo. It wasn't much, but then it was about as good as it got in this rough country. Longarm spied a livery up ahead, and rode in to see if he could learn more about Dottie.

"Yeah," the owner of the livery said, "I stabled her horse in the barn and directed her over to Mrs. Hoskins' boardinghouse where she'd be safe to spend the night. That gal sure is a little thing, ain't she?"

"She is."

"Pretty as a picture, though. She your runaway daughter or something?"

"Hell, no!"

"I didn't mean any offense, Marshal. It's just that the girl only looks about thirteen or fourteen years old."

Not if you'd seen her undressed and seen how she can make love, Longarm wanted to say, but kept the thought to himself.

"I'll put my horse up here too," he decided. "Where is Mrs. Hoskins's place?"

"It's that yellow-frame house with all the roses out in front about a block up the street. Can't miss it."

"Thanks."

"But it's a boardinghouse only for women. Mrs. Hoskins is pretty strict about even letting a man inside. Any visiting you do would have to be on the front porch or in town."

"The front porch would suit me fine," Longarm said, well remembering that he and Dottie had spent an unforgettable evening making love on Rebecca's front porch.

It was about eight o'clock when Longarm arrived at the boardinghouse. He could hear women's laughter and piano music inside, and had to knock quite loudly before a matronly woman with gray hair and a pleasantly plump face appeared.

"What is it?" she asked with obvious annoyance. "Everyone knows I don't allow my ladies to accept gentlemen callers after dinner."

"I'm a federal marshal and I need to see Dorothy Quigley."

"What for?"

"It's personal, ma'am."

"Let me see your badge, young man. You don't look very presentable."

"I've ridden a long, hard way to overtake Miss Quigley." Longarm extracted his badge and pressed it up against the still-locked screen door. "It's very important that I talk to her right now."

"Very well," the woman said with reluctance after studying his badge, "but federal officer or not, you really ought to bathe and shave before calling on a young lady like Miss Quigley. It's disrespectful to appear looking so unkempt."

Longarm removed his hat and bowed. "Mrs. Hoskins, I sincerely apologize."

The apology did the trick. "Please wait just a moment. Miss Quigley is resting in her room. Is the poor dear in some awful fix?"

"Nothing too serious."

"I had a feeling something was wrong when she arrived looking tired and discouraged. I hope you can help her."

"I'm going to try."

"Good."

Longarm was weary and pretty discouraged himself about the events of the previous disastrous day and night. He wanted a couple of drinks, a cigar, and a good night's sleep, and was determined to have them after talking sense into Dottie.

"How did you find me?"

He had turned his back to the door, and was gazing up at the stars when she surprised him by this sudden question. Longarm turned around and saw that Dottie wore a pink dress and her raven-colored hair was tied up on her head, making her look like a fairy-tale princess.

"Dottie, I make my living finding missing persons."

"You should not have bothered."

"I come to tell you how sorry I am about Gazella."

"Are you actually going to make up an excuse?"

"No. I was weak and have no defense for my behavior."

Dottie's lower lip trembled, and he heard the pain she felt when she said, "Custis, I have no claim of any kind on you. And I realize that we aren't married or engaged or anything, but—but, well, I thought we had something special between us!''

''We do.'' He stepped forward and gathered Dottie in his arms. ''We have something very special. That's why I can't allow you to return to Pine and your husband.''

Longarm heard her sharp intake of breath and felt her stiffen. ''So you know about my past,'' she said.

''Yes. Part of it anyway. But probably not all.''

Dottie extracted herself and walked over to the porch swing. She sat down and motioned Longarm to sit beside her. ''This is difficult,'' she said, ''but you need to understand.''

''I'm a good listener.''

''All right. I fell in love with a young mustanger named Jared Tanner. He was not one of our faith, but he'd been severely injured and was brought to my husband's household, where we set his broken bones and cared for him until he recovered. When it was time for Jared to leave, we both plotted to escape together.''

''But something went very wrong.''

''Yes.'' Dottie sighed deeply. ''My husband found out about our plan somehow, and the next thing I knew, I got a note from Jared saying he had sinned by tempting a married woman. He said that he had regained his senses and gone to Central City, where he had a job waiting with his father.''

''Then he must not have been really in love with you.''

''Oh, yes, he was! Jared was forced to leave at gunpoint unless I'm badly mistaken. And forced to write that letter. He would never have used the word 'sinned'!''

''How can you be so certain?''

''Because Jared despised religious zealots with a passion just as I do. To him, sin was no more than a word created by those people in order to make everyone feel guilty.''

"Do you think that is where he went?"

"I'm sure of it. He talked of his father many times, and how he owned a mining claim and had pleaded with Jared to help him come and work it. I was headed for Central City when I fell on hard times and stopped off to recover a bit at my uncle's place. I was broke, sick, and desperate.''

"Why were you going to Pine?"

"I felt that I had to talk with my husband and end this marriage. I didn't want Jared to ever fear being arrested as a bigamist or have someone come after him with a gun and try to take me back.''

"They might do that?"

"Of course! My husband is a very stubborn man. Once he believes he has claim to something—a horse, land, a wife—he will never let go without a fight.''

"Bigamy isn't recognized in Colorado. You are free here.''

"I know that. My uncle told me the same thing, but I just didn't think it was fair to Jared to have that shadow hanging over us. I was willing to do whatever it took to be truly free.''

"I suspect you would have failed and not been allowed to ever leave your husband's house again.''

"You might be correct. And to be honest, I am completely confused now. I love Jared, and then you came into my life and . . . well, I'm sure I've been very foolish.''

"And so have I," Longarm said, realizing he was jealous of Jared Tanner and not at all clear of his own feelings. "Is your uncle involved with Henry Tilson in this extortion thing that is going on back at Goldstrike?''

''No. He's a hard man, but a fair one. He has no more use for Tilson than I do.''

''And your cousin, Delbert?''

''He was involved with Tilson, although I'm not sure how. Delbert frightened me. He would have been useful to Tilson and your friend as far as putting fear into the people that they fleeced.''

Longarm shook his head. ''I feel terrible about Wade being involved in something like extortion, but I'll always think of him as a good, courageous lawman.''

''We all make mistakes,'' Dottie said. ''I guess my going back to Utah would have been a pretty bad one, huh?''

''Yes. But I'd have gone to Pine and rescued you.'' Longarm decided to tell Dottie about his own mistake. ''Tilson tried to arrest me just as I was about to come looking for you.''

''Why?''

''He needed a scapegoat. Someone to blame for the murders so that he could look as if he were a successful marshal. What better person than me, the one who has sworn to find out the truth.''

''So what happened?''

''He gave me no choice but to draw on him. He shot first, but I shot straightest, and he was down and hurt when someone else opened fire on me. I had to leave Goldstrike in a big hurry, and so I stole a horse.''

''You did?''

''It was either that or be shot down.''

''Any idea who was shooting?''

''No,'' Longarm replied, ''but I think that the gunfire was coming from in front of Dirty Dan's Saloon.''

''Well, that makes sense.''

148

"Why?"

"Because I'm sure that I saw Delbert and Dan together a number of times, and it wouldn't surprise me a whit to find out that they were in cahoots with the marshals."

"I'll check on that," Longarm promised.

Dottie looked back inside. "This is a nice boardinghouse, but I'll get my things and we'll find another place, if you like."

"I'm real tired, and Mrs. Hoskins told me I need a bath. Maybe I'll just come around in the morning."

"And then?"

"We'll go get Rebecca and Faith and I'll take you all to Central City, then come back and solve these murders."

"No," Dottie said. "That's too much trouble. Why don't I just sneak into Rebecca's place and then you can do what is necessary."

"I'll give it some thought," Longarm promised.

"If I know Rebecca, she's not going to stand for you dumping us off in Central City any more than I will."

"We've both had long, hard rides today," Longarm said. "I'll see you tomorrow morning and maybe we can think this out better with some rest."

Dottie lightly kissed his lips. "Are you as confused as I am?"

"Probably more so," he replied with a weary smile.

"Tomorrow morning then," she said. "I'll be waiting for you right here on this porch."

"Why is it that we are always meeting up on someone else's porch?"

"I don't know. Perhaps we should get married and have our own porch."

Longarm laughed, tipped his hat, and said, "Good night."

Chapter 14

It would take them two days to get back to Goldstrike, and while they were both happy to be together again, something had changed in their relationship. Why? Longarm knew they were worried about Rebecca and her baby as well as what would happen when they returned to Goldstrike, but he suspected Jared Tanner was also an important factor.

"I'm sorry," Dottie told him beside a dancing stream while their horses rested and grazed after a long uphill climb. "I don't know what to think anymore of us or Jared."

"You need time to sort out your feelings," Longarm answered. "Dottie, you've been under a lot of strain for a long time."

"So have you. And I've often wondered how you feel about your best friend becoming dishonest."

"I feel bad. Wade had changed a great deal in the last few years. I don't know why, but he lost something special. I think Rebecca saw that too."

"Does she . . ."

"No," Longarm said, anticipating Dottie's question. "Or at least I don't think she knows that Wade had

151

turned crooked, and I'd sooner die than tell her.''

"Of course. Why sully her husband's reputation?"

"Exactly. That's another reason I'd like to get her to Denver as soon as possible."

"Are you in love with Rebecca Crockett?"

Longarm failed in an attempt at laughter because the question was one that he had asked himself many times over the past years. "Dottie, that's an odd question."

"I don't think so. I'm sure plenty of men are in love with their best friends' wives or sweethearts. I know that I was in love with my sister's boyfriend for quite a while. However, he was eighteen and I was—oh, about ten."

"That would be a problem."

"Not as much as you might think when you are surrounded by Mormon polygamists. They form attachments young. But anyway, we were talking about you and Rebecca."

"I feel responsible for her, being as how both of her parents died a few years ago and she has no close living relatives." Longarm shrugged his broad shoulders. "I've always been Rebecca's friend and a bit jealous of Wade's good fortune."

"Do you think you could be happy if you married her?"

Longarm squirmed, and was feeling uncomfortable. "I thought we were talking about *us*?"

"We are. Please answer my question."

"I . . ." Longarm had to sort it out for a couple of seconds, and even then he wasn't certain that he had it right. "I feel *responsible* for taking care of Rebecca and Faith. If I had been married and then killed, I am sure that Wade would have felt the same way about my family."

"I see." Dottie smiled. "Well, don't become confused over the difference between love and responsibility. They go hand in hand, but they are definitely not one and the same emotion."

"I suppose not." Longarm stood up, knowing it was time to go. "I'll catch our horses."

"I'm sorry I bought yours without permission and you had to steal another."

"I would have had to anyway, in order to get out of Goldstrike alive. The bullets were really flying."

"I'm very worried about what will happen to you in Goldstrike."

"I'll be fine," Longarm replied with more assurance than he actually felt. "Let's ride."

They arrived back at Rebecca's house late the second night, and that was exactly as Longarm preferred, as there would probably be a warrant out for his arrest. He also knew that he was going to see Dirty Dan and see if he could get the saloon owner to confess his role, whatever it was, in the murders. It wouldn't be easy and it wouldn't be legal, but Longarm was determined to get whatever information he could from the man and then build on it until he had solved Wade's murder.

"I was so worried about the pair of you!" Rebecca said after they'd tied their horses in her barn and sneaked up to her back door. "You shouldn't have returned!"

Dottie hugged her and then said, "How is Faith?"

"She's fine, and she's not the one that I am worried about. Custis, do you know that you are a wanted man?"

"Sure. I stole a horse and then I shot the local marshal, so it doesn't surprise me one bit."

"You should rest a few hours and eat, then leave," Rebecca told him. "I'd die if you were caught and hanged!"

"That won't happen."

"You don't know Henry Tilson. He's playing the role of martyr, and has gained the sympathy of a lot of people in this town."

"I was afraid of that." Longarm hugged Rebecca, then said, "I'll be back soon."

"Where are you going!" Rebecca cried.

"First, I'm going to return the horse I stole to the hitching rail where it was tied. Then, I'm going to wait until I can catch Dirty Dan either coming or going from his saloon and force him to confess his role in the murders."

"He's a tough man," Rebecca said. "Even my husband was afraid to cross him unless it was an absolute necessity."

"This is an 'absolute necessity,' " Longarm told her. "I have to have a break in this case, and fast, or I'm facing a hanging."

"Can I help?" Dottie asked.

"You can take my horse back to Buck Beller's livery right now without being seen by anyone. Tell the man to keep him inside the barn where he won't be noticed and that I'll pay him a little extra for his trouble and his silence."

"I'll do that," Dottie promised. "Then what?"

"Come back here and stay out of sight. I'll return before dawn, hopefully with a confession from Dirty Dan."

"I think he'll prefer to fight before talking," Rebecca said. "Especially if he's had a hand in the murders of Wade and poor Irwin Duggan."

154

"We'll see. If that is his choice, then at least I'll know that I got Wade's killer."

"I'll get some food warmed up, and then you rest," Rebecca said as Dottie went out the door to return Longarm's horse to Beller's livery.

"Buck!" Dottie called when she arrived at the livery a short time later. "Mr. Beller?"

"Who the hell is a'wakin' me up at this hour of the night?"

Dottie cleared her throat. "It's Dottie Quigley. You remember, I used to work for my uncle, Mr. Iverson."

"Hold on while I get dressed," the liveryman groused. "I expect that this couldn't wait until morning."

"No, sir."

Buck appeared several minutes later with three or four sleepy-eyed cats in tow. "Well, little lady," the ex-cowboy said, holding up a lantern and staring owlishly. "Let's hear your sad story."

In as few words as necessary, Dottie told him how Custis had overtaken her and that they'd returned to try to solve the murders of Marshal Crockett and Irwin Duggan. She ended by saying, "We know that it's risky, but . . ."

"Risky?" Buck gave her a good laugh. "Young woman, if they catch your big friend, they'll have a necktie party for certain! Everyone in this town except a few of us with more sense and better memories has put Marshal Tilson on a pedestal. They forget that he is as crooked as a dog's hind leg."

"What about Dirty Dan?"

The question seemed to catch him off guard. "Dirty Dan?"

155

"That's right. Rebecca—I mean, Mrs. Crockett and I both think that he is tied into this somehow."

"That wouldn't surprise me a bit," Buck said. "Dan would sell his mother for a dollar and a beer."

"Marshal Long is going to try and catch him by surprise, then get him off alone somewhere and make him confess his part, if any, in the awful murders of Mr. Crockett and Duggan."

"Why not just get Tilson to confess?"

Dottie shrugged. "I suppose because he carries a badge."

"Yeah," Buck agreed. "I see how that could make a big difference. Anything I could do to help?"

"Maybe. You know this town better than any of us. Where does Dan live?"

"He's got a house up the street a couple of doors from his saloon. He doesn't live alone, though. Always has one of his . . . ladies of the night staying with him."

"I see." Dottie bit her lower lip. "I sure am worried about Custis."

"Why'd you run off like you did?"

"It's a long story, Mr. Beller, but I'm glad to say that I didn't get where I was headed and I'm back here to help Mrs. Crockett and her baby and help Custis solve these murders."

"I'd like to do my part as well," Buck said. "If I don't, this town is going to hell in a handcart. Right now it's the prostitutes and the gamblers that are getting fleeced, but it won't stop there. Sooner or later, Tilson or Dan or someone like them will come here to me and demand money every week for protection. And when that happens, I'm either going to shoot them dead or be shot dead."

"It doesn't have to come to that."

"I know," Buck said, hitching up his pants and then picking up a noisy tabby cat and stroking it quiet. "And that's why I'm willing to do whatever I can to help that federal marshal."

"Maybe you can tell us more about Dirty Dan."

"Nope. He's one of them fellas that I've managed to keep at a good distance. He told me once that he don't like animals, especially cats, so I knew he was a bad one through and through. You like cats, don't you?"

"Oh, yes," Dottie said, picking up a black and white cat and hugging it close. "I like them a lot."

"I guessed it." Buck expelled a deep breath. "I suppose you'd like me to keep the marshal's horse out of sight, huh?"

"That's right."

"When you see him next, wish him well and tell him he can come here to hide if need be and that I'll do whatever I can to help."

"Custis will appreciate that, and probably pay you some extra for your trouble."

"Listen," Buck said, "if he puts a stop to Tilson and whoever else is in cahoots with him, then I won't charge him a cent for putting up his horse. You tell him that, will you?"

"Yes, sir!"

Dottie handed the reins to Buck, and then placed her cat on the floor. "I'll be seeing him soon, and I'll also tell him where you said Dirty Dan lives and that he never sleeps alone."

"Say," Buck said, turning around. "It ain't my business and I sure have no right to ask, but was you really a Mormon fella's wife?"

"I was. One of eight."

"Any more like you? I mean some older, but as brave, hardworkin', and almost as pretty?"

"I'm afraid not."

Buck shook his head. "Damn shame that a few men get to have so many wives while a fella like me can't even get one for hisself!"

"It is a shame. Maybe someday you'll find a perfect wife."

"I hope so, but she's going to have to love cats and horses about as much as I do in order to stand this situation."

"You'll still find her."

"Thanks. Tell the marshal howdy and I'm ready, willin', and maybe even able to help."

"I'll do that!"

When Dottie returned to the Crockett house, Longarm was already stretched out asleep in the extra bedroom. Rebecca was sitting in her kitchen rocking Faith and humming a gospel tune.

"Mr. Beller says he's ready, willing, and maybe even able to help us if we need him."

"That's good," Rebecca answered, "because we just might. Did he put Custis's horse in a stall where it won't be seen?"

"Yes." Dottie went over and took the baby from Rebecca, saying, "You look real tired."

"I am, but you must be as well. You've ridden a long ways."

"I was stupid to have tried to return and fix things up in Utah with my husband. I can see that now, but at the time I left, I was just real upset with Custis for . . . well, seeing Gazella."

"I won't make excuses for Custis, but Gazella is a very persistent and insistent woman. I've learned a lot

158

about her that I wish I didn't know just since Custis has arrived.''

"I asked Mr. Beller if he thought Dirty Dan might be in league with Marshal Iverson, and he said yes.''

"I don't know the man.''

"I don't either, but he sure looks tough.''

"Custis will change all that in a hurry,'' Rebecca predicted. "When he gets serious with a man he doesn't like or suspects is guilty of a serious crime, Custis can strike fear into his heart.''

"I'm sure that he can.''

Dottie began to rock the baby. "I missed Faith,'' she said with a tired smile. "Someday I hope to get married and have one just like this.''

"You will. Custis told me about your Utah polygamist husband and that young mustanger you fell in love with. He said he'd take you over to Central City on the way to Denver.''

"He sure wants you to go with him.''

"I know. But I'm going to have to give that some serious thought before I pull up stakes and go to Denver. I don't know a soul there anymore.''

"You know Custis,'' Dottie said.

"Yes, I do. And that means I need to remind myself that his work will always come first. Custis loves the excitement and adventure and he takes his oath of office very seriously. Any woman who thinks she can lasso and tie him down is badly mistaken.''

Dottie knew those words were spoken as a warning that she should guard her heart. "Maybe *you* could make him settle down a mite.''

"I doubt that.''

"Rebecca, he thinks the world of you and this baby girl.''

"Sure, he does. I have no doubt that Custis would give his life to protect us all. But he'd do the same for a complete stranger who was about to be hurt or killed. That's just his code of honor. It's what he has sworn to do. And while you may not believe this, Wade would have done the same."

Dottie nodded, not sure if she believed that, but certainly not willing to argue the point.

"You see," Rebecca was saying, "men are a lot different from women. Now, I'm not going to lecture, and I know that there are plenty of things that you could tell me, but I have given this matter a great deal of thought and I do know the mentality of a good lawman."

"Which is?"

"They'll always defend the innocent, the weak, the injured to the death against a bully or aggressor. But they might also be tempted by a bribe and convince themselves that there are exceptions to every rule. Lawmen can, if they are not very careful, began to make their own laws. To lose the distinction between what is lawful and not lawful and instead become their own judge and jury."

"Is that what happened to your husband?"

"He was tempted by money, and he probably was sure that taking a few dollars here and there in order to take care of me and his newborn justified breaking a few rules. It didn't, of course, but I'm sure that's what he thought."

"Did you ever discuss this with him?"

"I—I tried. He would become incensed and start shouting that I should mind my own business. I was pregnant, of course, and worried that getting too upset might cause me to lose my baby. It had happened before, and so I was willing to keep the peace at any price, which was, of course, wrong.''

"Even if it allowed you to have Faith?"

"I don't know." Rebecca sighed. "Why don't we just all lie down and say a little prayer that everything will turn out all right. That good and truth will prevail and that we will go on to lead long, happy lives."

"I think that is a wonderful idea," Dottie said as she looked down at the sleeping babe in her arms.

Chapter 15

Longarm awakened about midnight, quietly dressed, and prepared to leave without waking the women—or Baby Faith, who was sleeping soundly in her crib. His intention was to return the horse he'd stolen, and then watch Dirty Dan's Saloon and see if he could waylay and then force important information from its proprietor.

But he awakened Dottie while tiptoeing to the back door and bumping into a chair.

"Hey, wait," she whispered, hurrying to his side. "I need to tell you something."

"I'm listening."

"I talked to Buck Beller, and he said that Dan lives just a couple of doors down the street. Says he's always got one of his women with him at night."

"I'll check there first," Longarm decided. "Why don't you go back to sleep?"

"I'll try," Dottie promised with a yawn. "Are you sure that you have to do this?"

"Yes. I'm running out of time. If I don't get some kind of break soon, I'll have to return to Denver after delivering you to Central City."

"I'm not sure that I can leave Rebecca and Faith to make their own way here in Goldstrike."

"You have to do what you think best," Longarm answered, checking his gun and pulling his hat down as low as possible over his face.

"One more thing I should tell you," she said.

"And that is?"

"Buck Beller also said that if you got in trouble, you could hide out at his livery. He hates both Marshal Tilson and Dirty Dan. I asked him if they might be in cahoots in these murders, and he thought it was possible."

"I'll keep that in mind," Longarm told her. "Now go back to bed and get some sleep."

Dottie stretched up on her tiptoes and kissed Longarm. "That's for love and luck."

"Thanks!"

As he moved outside, Longarm felt better for having taken a nap. His mind was clearer and his purpose more focused. He needed to get to Dan and pressure him hard enough to get a confession. That would be no small trick because the saloon owner was obviously not a man who would be easily intimidated. If Dan were guilty of extortion and murder, he would even be harder to crack.

Longarm made his way to the barn, where the horse he'd stolen was still saddled. He'd grained the animal heavily, and it was somewhat worse for wear after its long pursuit of Dottie, but it would soon recover. Longarm tightened the cinch, bridled the tall horse, and mounted. He rode up the main street of Goldstrike with his chin resting on his chest. The more popular saloons were still doing a good business, but there was almost no one on horseback at this late hour. A few noisy drunks were loafing on the boardwalk, finishing their whiskey and lies for the night, when Longarm rode up to the hitching rail and dismounted.

"Say there, mister!" one of them shouted. "You're kinda getting a late start on the night, ain't ya?"

"I guess," Longarm muttered.

"That's a mighty tall and handsome horse you're rid-in'," another offered. "Better tie him up good. A fella had a horse like him stolen just a couple days ago from that very hitchin' rail."

They seemed to find the act of horse theft hilarious, and began to howl with drunken laughter. Longarm paid them no mind. He was counting on the fact that none of these men owned this particular animal and that therefore, news of its return would not get around until tomorrow morning. And by then, he hoped to have solved the mystery of who killed Wade Crockett and Irwin Duggan.

Longarm strolled up the street, and came to what had to be Dirty Dan's ramshackle house. It sure wasn't much, and he walked by slowly, looking for a light inside but not seeing one. That meant either that Dan was still tending bar at his saloon, or he was inside and already asleep. Longarm hoped that the latter was the case. The quickest way to find out, of course, would be to travel the very short distance to the man's saloon, look inside, and see if Dan was still pouring whiskey behind his plank bar. But that would also be the most dangerous move, because someone might recognize him and then all hell would break loose.

So what to do? Longarm decided to circle Dan's house and sneak inside. If he could do that, then he could either catch the man asleep or wait to jump him. A quick blow to the side of the big man's head, and then Longarm needed only to silence one of Dan's girls in order to get the situation under his control.

Thanks to ample moonlight, Longarm had no trouble locating the back of Dan's house or navigating his way through a backyard littered with piles of rusting tin cans and empty whiskey bottles. It was obvious that Dan took no more pride in his house than in his saloon. The only unexpected complication was a skinny brown mongrel dog tied to Dan's back door. Longarm frowned, wondering if the animal would raise a ruckus or even try to bite him.

"Hello there," he whispered when the dog rushed to the end of its tether rope and then stood watching. "How's it going this fine evening."

The dog whined.

"I won't hurt you. Looks like you've missed a lot of meals."

Suddenly, the dog rolled over onto its back in an attitude of complete submission. Longarm crawled forward and laid a hand on its side, and was rewarded by a severe tongue-licking. "Some watchdog you are, poor girl."

He crouched beside the female and stroked her chest, deciding that the poor starving beast had probably been beaten until it was nearly worthless. The dog kept licking his hand, and he wished he had some food to give it in return.

"Is he home?" Longarm whispered. "Is Dirty Dan home?"

The dog whined softly and jumped up, desperate for more petting. Longarm had to extricate himself from the pathetic animal, and then struggle to keep it from leaping through the door when he slipped inside. He could still hear it whining pitifully as he made his way through the dim kitchen, smelling the rank odor of decaying food.

He lit a match, and it took him only a few minutes to determine that Dan hadn't returned yet. Longarm went back into the kitchen and found an icebox, and opened it to discover a couple of thick steaks. With a satisfied smile, he opened the back door and fed them to the starving dog. She gulped the first one down without even bothering to chew. Tail swinging like a leafless branch in a high mountain wind, the dog slowed down to eat the second steak, and its tail never stopped wagging.

"I hate people who abuse women, children, and animals," he told the grateful dog as he knelt beside the kitchen and looked up at the moon. "I think you would be far better off turned free and left to your own devices than to be tied here and slowly starved to death."

The dog finished the second steak, and Longarm would have cut the rope that was knotted around its neck and set it free, except that he was afraid it might run around to the front of the house and alert Dan that something was wrong. On the other hand, if things went really bad, maybe this would be a final act of kindness.

"Oh, hell," he said, taking out his pocketknife and cutting the dog's rope.

She actually yipped with what sounded to Longarm like pure joy. "All right now," he said, "this is your chance, so make a run for it. Find someone who will treat you much better!"

But the dog wouldn't leave. Instead of taking off as he'd expected, it sat down on its skinny haunches, belched loudly, and then whined for more petting.

"Sorry," Longarm said, going back inside. He found a big stuffed chair and sat down to wait for the arrival of Dan, which, he figured, should not be long.

Maybe he dozed off, because he awakened with a start

to hear Dan shout, "Gawdammit, dog, did you chew through that rope again!"

The animal whimpered, and Longarm heard Dan curse. The curse was followed by a sharp yip of pain and then: "Get the hell out of here if you want to go so bad! Take off, you worthless cur! I'll find a *real* watchdog!"

"Oh, Dan, don't be so mean to her. Come here, Willow!"

Longarm heard Willow's tail bouncing up and down on the front porch, then Dan's key scraping in the key lock. He was furious at the big man for hurting a dog that, despite the worst kind of ill treatment, still remained a faithful pet. He could not understand why Willow would wait for her cruel master.

And so, Dan, it seems you like to beat and starve helpless animals, Longarm thought grimly. *Well, maybe it's time that you tasted a little of your own medicine.*

That was Longarm's frame of mind when Dan pushed inside, followed by one of his prostitutes. Longarm could have used his fist, but fearing to break a knuckle against the big man's lantern jaw, he pistol-whipped Dan hard enough to drop him like a rock on his filthy floor. The woman must have had plenty to drink, because she just stared dumbly at Longarm for a moment in shock and confusion. Before she could recover and scream or try to escape, Longarm pushed her painted face into the sofa chair, found a piece of cording coming loose from the chair, and used it to tie her hands behind her back.

"Scream and I'll put you to sleep like Dan," he warned.

She was nearly as skinny and pathetic as the dog named Willow. "Don't hit me," she cried. "Please don't hit me. I ain't got nothing worth taking. And if you want a ride, then just lift my skirt and do it! But please don't—''

''I won't hurt you if you stay quiet.''

''Are you going to kill Dirty Dan?''

''No, but I'm going to find out if he knows who killed Marshal Crockett and Irwin Duggan.''

''He won't tell you anything! You can kill him and he won't tell ya that it was his—oops!''

''His what?''

''Never mind. I'm drunk.''

''Who were you about to say killed them?''

''I don't know!''

Longarm didn't want to do it, but he dug his pocket-knife out and then yanked her head back. ''I'm going to cut your throat from ear to ear if you don't tell me the truth.''

The prostitute tried to scream, but he clamped his hand over her mouth. ''Tell me who killed Wade Crockett and the drunk, Irwin Duggan, and stuffed his body in the pile of straw!''

''Tilson killed your friend Marshal Crockett!''

Longarm eased her head forward a little. ''Why?''

''Dan said that Marshal Crockett wanted to stop taking our money. He got cold feet and felt guilty or something even as they were really starting to rake in the cash.''

''Let me get this straight. Wade had a change of heart and wanted to stop taking money off the gamblers and saloon women?''

''Yes, but please don't kill me.''

''So who killed old Irwin Duggan?''

''Please don't make me tell you!''

''Why not!''

''I'll be killed!''

"You'll be killed quicker if you don't tell me right now."

"All right, Dan did!"

"Why?"

"He was afraid Duggan would learn something that would send him to the gallows, so he followed him out of the saloon one night and killed him out behind Buck Beller's livery."

"How do you know that?"

"He was seen leaving. There was some straw on his pants the next day. Marshal, I ain't no genius, but I can add two plus two and tell you that it was Dirty Dan what killed poor old Duggan."

Longarm nodded. It all made sense, and he'd bet anything that Dirty Dan's boots matched the big footprints he'd measured at the murder site.

"Can you write?"

"Huh?"

"I need a written statement saying what you've just told me."

"Dan would kill me!"

"I'm a United States deputy marshal. I'll arrest and take both Dan and Tilson to Denver for trial. I promise you they will be sent to prison longer than you'll even hope to live unless you find a new line of work."

Tears streamed down the woman's ruined face, smearing her heavy makeup. "You promise?"

"You have my word on it."

"I don't believe in promises, Marshal. Men have been promisin' me things all my life and failin' to deliver."

"You have no choice now but to do as I ask. If you don't and I fail to send Dan and Tilson to prison for lack of evidence, they will hunt you down and kill you slow."

She sniffled. "Would you really have cut my throat?"

"No, I was bluffing."

"All right then. I'll do what you ask."

"Good! Now let's see if we can find a paper and pen in this pigsty."

Minutes later, Longarm had a written statement signed by Irma Jones. "Irma," he said, "you can go now."

"Where?"

"I don't care, as long as you don't leave Goldstrike."

"What are you going to do with Dirty Dan?"

"I'm going to wake him up and get a confession."

"He won't—"

"He has no choice now that I have your signed statement," Longarm told her. "But I do think it would be better for you to leave right now."

Irma staggered to the front door and Willow was waiting, all excited and yipping with glee.

"Do you want his dog?" Longarm asked.

"My life ain't suited to a dog. I live worse than this dog."

"Then let her inside and I'll find her a home."

"Willow is a sweet girl," Irma said. "I hope you treat her well."

"I promise that her life is about to improve," Longarm said as the dog rushed into the room and licked his hand, then the blood seeping out of Dirty Dan's scalp.

"Marshal?"

"Yeah?"

"Will I have to go to Denver and tell a judge what I told you?"

"No, not unless you want to."

"If you paid my way, I'd come."

"I'll pay your way, Irma. Now go and don't say a word to anyone."

"I sure won't! You don't set him free or I'm dead."

"I understand."

"What are you—"

"Irma, git!"

She hurried off, and Longarm took Willow in his arms and said, "Let's go see if we can find anything more for you to eat."

Willow seemed more than pleased at the prospect, and so Longarm followed her swinging tail into the cluttered kitchen.

Chapter 16

Longarm had Dirty Dan hog-tied by the time he revived, and it was a good thing because the saloon owner woke up fighting mad.

"If you don't settle down, I'm going to give you another tap on the noggin," Longarm warned as he fed Willow the last of the meat he'd found in the kitchen's icebox. "And Dan, I guarantee it will put you out a lot longer than this first blow."

"What the hell are you doin' bustin' into my house! And stay away from my damned dog."

"I don't think Willow wants to be your dog anymore," Longarm answered as Willow sat close beside him, thumping her tail on the floor and licking her chops.

"Where is that skinny whore Irma?"

"She's gone."

Longarm lit a cigar and leaned back in the big easy chair, stroking Willow's head. "You don't have much use for gals like Irma or dogs that you can bully and beat, do you?"

"What the hell is it to you!" Dan winced because of his outburst. "Damn, you must have opened up my skull."

"I know that you killed poor Duggan and stuffed him into that pile of straw behind Buck Beller's livery."

"Just try and prove it."

"I found little pieces of straw on this floor."

"That don't mean a damn thing! No court in the country will convict me with that kind of stupid evidence."

"I've got a statement here," Longarm said, holding it up and waving it before the saloon owner's eyes. "It says that you murdered Duggan to keep him from finding out evidence and collecting my reward. This written statement, along with the sworn testimony of its author, will definitely send you to the gallows."

"Whose statement!"

"Irma's."

"Ha! No one will believe a damned whore."

"Oh, yes, they will," Longarm said as he unfolded a piece of paper in the outline of a footprint. He leaned over and placed it against the sole of Dan's boot. "Perfect fit."

"What . . ."

"I took your footprint from the murder site, and it is a perfect match, just as expected."

Dan's eyes flicked from his feet to the outline and back again. "That don't prove nothing. Plenty of other people have big feet."

"Maybe, but I'll testify that your heel mark also matches the tracks I found behind the livery barn." Longarm smiled. "You add that, the loose straw, and Irma's statement, and I'm quite sure we can help the Denver hangman earn his living."

"Denver?"

"You heard me." Although tired and gritty-eyed from this long night, Longarm was thoroughly enjoying himself. "You're going to Denver for trial because I'm sure that you and Tilson have the local circuit judge on your payroll. Am I right?"

"Listen, Marshal Tilson is the law in Goldstrike. You've got no right to arrest and take me to Denver or anywhere else. You're out of line!"

"If you're suggesting that I might receive a mild reprimand for overstepping my authority, I guess you are probably correct," Longarm agreed. "But when I watch you do the dance of death, kicking like crazy at the end of a noose, it will all seem worthwhile."

Dirty Dan swallowed hard. It appeared to Longarm as if the man was finally starting to realize that this was no bluff.

"Ahh, now see here, Marshal Long, I—I ain't sure that you know the half of what went on in Goldstrike."

Longarm shrugged. "I know you killed Duggan. I'm also sure that you killed my friend, Marshal Crockett."

"I didn't kill him!"

"Of course you did."

"No!" Dan gulped again. "Maybe we could strike a deal."

"I don't make deals."

"But I didn't kill your marshal friend."

"Then you'd better tell me who did, or you'll be charged with his murder."

"You've no proof. You *couldn't* have proof because I'm innocent of that killing."

"Maybe and maybe not, but just the fact that you'll be charged with it is going to make things even worse for you in the eyes of a judge and jury. So what if I can't make that charge stick? It'll still be worth my time to try just to make sure you dance in a hangman's noose."

Dan closed his eyes, and sweat began to roll down his face. "What if I cooperate?"

"How?"

"By telling you everything. Any chance that I could get off free?"

"Nope."

"Then what about just going to prison and not getting hanged? Dammit, Marshal, you got to see it from my point of view and help me out!"

Longarm's voice hardened. "Why? I've no doubt that I can get you convicted and hanged for killing that poor drunken Duggan. What do I need to worry about whether or not a jury finds you guilty of also killing Wade? Either way, your neck still gets stretched."

"Don't keep saying that! I can't stand the idea of hanging. I've seen it happen a couple times, and it's awful."

"It isn't pretty," Longarm agreed.

"Prison," Dirty Dan begged. "How about I tell you who killed your friend, Marshal Crockett, and you see if you can get me life in prison?"

"You'd have to tell me who ambushed Wade and then sign a statement."

"If I did that, would you try to keep me from getting hanged?"

"No promises."

"But would you give me your word that you'd at least *try* to keep me from hanging?"

"All right, I'll try."

"How can I be sure you will keep your word?"

"You'll just have to trust me."

"Dammit, that ain't good enough! I don't trust nobody, not even my mother, who goes to church every day down in Taos."

"Sorry, but it's the best you'll get from me. Now, shall I find a paper and pencil for you to write out exactly how my friend was murdered and who pulled the trigger, or is this conversation finished?"

"Get the paper and pencil," Dan choked in bitter defeat. "I'll put down that Deputy Henry Tilson shot Crockett."

"Why?"

"I'm sure you can figure that out."

"Tell me anyway."

"Tilson wanted to be marshal, and besides that, Crockett was getting soft. He wanted to go straight just when they were starting to make big money."

"That's what Irma said."

"That rotten bitch!"

"At least she didn't murder a poor drunk," Longarm snapped as he got the writing materials.

An hour later, Longarm had Dan in jail, and was making a fresh pot of coffee and reading yesterday's paper in Wade's old office chair.

"Say, Dan, what time does Tilson usually arrive here in the morning?"

"How should I know?"

"Well," Longarm said, "whenever he comes, we'll be ready."

"I hope he shoots you dead."

Longarm smiled at the man who sat looking angry and defeated in the jail cell. "Sure, you do. That would save your hide until Tilson found your confession and statement resting on his desk. What do you think he

177

might do to you after learning he was double-crossed? You think of that yet?''

Clearly, Dirty Dan *hadn't* thought of it, because he sucked in his breath and grew pale.

Longarm dozed off and on through the remainder of the long night. Willow sometimes awakened him by licking his hand. That was fine, and he scratched her behind the ears.

''This is a good dog,'' Longarm called out as the first rays of daylight began to brighten their front window. ''Who would take care of a fine, loyal, and loving animal like Willow?''

''Nobody. That's just a flea-bitten mongrel I picked up thinkin' she might make a good watchdog. Which she didn't! I hope the bitch starves to death after I'm gone.''

''Not a chance,'' Longarm replied. ''We're going to find Willow a new and much better home. Any ideas?''

''Why should I care what happens to it?''

''No reason, I guess.''

''You're talking about a cur and I'm worrying about my life!'' Dan shouted through the bar cells. ''What kind of a hard-nosed sonofabitch are you?''

''I'm a federal marshal that is about to slam the door on Henry Tilson's coffin,'' Longarm answered, jabbing a forefinger at the street. ''And you are going to see it all happen when he comes through that door.''

''Tilson is hurt bad, but there's nothing wrong with his gun hand, and I hope you both shoot each other plumb to death.''

''I guess that would solve your problems, huh?''

''Damn right it would.''

''Ain't gonna happen,'' Longarm said flatly as he scratched behind Willow's other floppy ear.

• • •

It was nearly ten o'clock when Longarm heard the marshal jam his key into the front-door lock. Over in the cell, Dan sat up suddenly, and he seemed to be trying to decide what to do next, warn Tilson or keep silent and let the cards fall where they may.

"Not one word," Longarm hissed to his prisoner as he lowered his boots to the floor and drew his six-gun. "Or I'll shut you up for keeps."

Dirty Dan muttered something under his breath, and lay back down with his ugly face turned to the door. Longarm knew that his prisoner really was hoping for a deadly shootout, but that wasn't likely.

Tilson pushed through the door, not even noticing Longarm, who had positioned himself behind Wade's desk.

"Morning, Marshal," Longarm said without warmth. "Put your hands up and don't try anything stupid or you're a dead man."

The keys spilled from Tilson's fist, and for just an instant, Longarm thought the fool was going to reach for his gun. But then, just as suddenly as the notion came, it left him.

"You can't get away with this!"

"Shut the door behind you."

Tilson slammed the door with the heel of his boot.

"Now put your hands up high," Longarm ordered, cocking back the hammer of his gun. "And keep them up."

"I'll have this town come down on your head and you'll soon be swinging from a tree limb."

"Maybe," Longarm replied, disarming the man and then searching him to make sure Tilson had no hidden

179

weapons before prodding him toward the jail cell. "Say, Dan, you've just got a new roommate!"

"What the hell are you doing in there!" Tilson shouted.

"What does it look like. He got the drop on me same as he did you."

"March," Longarm ordered, jamming Tilson in the spine.

When he got them both locked up, he said, "Tilson, you might as well understand what is happening. I've got a signed confession from your friend Dan saying that you murdered Marshal Wade Crockett."

"No!" Tilson turned on Dirty Dan. "You didn't do that, did you?"

"He doesn't want to hang," Longarm said. "And he would have if he hadn't done what I asked. 'Cause you see, I've got another sworn statement from Miss Irma Jones telling the court that Dirty Dan killed Irwin Duggan."

"You sonofabitch!" Tilson wailed to Dan. "I'll kill you!"

Longarm sat down in Wade's chair as Tilson attacked Dirty Dan. It was soon over. With a bullet wound in his side still healing and being the smaller of the pair, Henry Tilson didn't stand a chance against the larger, more powerful saloon owner. Dirty Dan beat the stuffing out of Tilson, and might even have killed him if Longarm hadn't put a stop to the fight.

"That's enough, Dan! You beat him to death and it will get you hanged for certain."

"I should never have listened to him in the first place!"

"That's true," Longarm said, moseying over to the cell and surveying the nearly unconscious Tilson. "It's a long way to Denver, so watch your back. I'll keep you both handcuffed, but he'll kill you if he gets the least little chance."

"I know that. But I'm going to keep him so beat up he won't have no chance at all. You still gonna try to keep me from the noose?"

"I will if you repeat what you've written in a Denver courtroom."

"I'll do that. What about my saloon?"

"Say good-bye to it."

Dirty Dan covered his whiskered face and wept like a baby.

Chapter 17

They were ready to leave Goldstrike. Rebecca had sold her house for a fair price, and Faith was bouncing on her knee as she sat in the big rented carriage that Longarm intended to drive all the way down to Denver in grand style. Irma Jones and Dottie had agreed to sit in the backseats with guns while Henry Tilson and Dirty Dan sat in the middle seat, handcuffed and shackled together as tight as a pair of calmshells.

Iverson and the other council members and town leaders looked grim as they prepared to watch much of their recent misery depart for Denver. Longarm had read aloud both statements concerning the exact circumstances regarding the murders of former Marshal Wade Crockett and Irwin Duggan.

"Where is Willow?" Longarm asked as he prepared to climb up beside Rebecca. "I've grown fond of that little mutt, and I'm not about to leave her fate to chance."

"Here she comes! Gazella's got her!"

It was true. Gazella had the little dog wrapped in her arms, and there were tears streaming down her rosy cheeks. "I—I was hoping you'd forget about Willow and leave her here with me. I sure love dogs and, well, with you leaving, I'm having a hard time right now facing being alone."

Rebecca looked at Longarm, rolling her eyes, and he was really glad he couldn't see Dottie's expression in the backseat. Most likely, she was trying not to laugh out loud.

"Bring the dog here," Longarm ordered.

Gazella brought it over, sniffling and looking as if she was giving up her only child.

"So long, both of you," Longarm said.

"What . . ."

"I can't keep a dog," Longarm said. "Rebecca has Faith and Dottie—what do you have, Dottie?"

"I have a man in Central City and another that I'm still not quite sure about marrying."

"You're referring to me?"

"I am."

Irma cried, "What about me? What have I got!"

"You've got a new and better life in Denver," Dottie told her. "If you want it. And, well, you're going to be pretty important in Denver when you testify."

"I am?"

"I'll bet so. Isn't that right, Custis?"

"That's right," he said, scratching Willow behind the ears, giving Gazella a kiss on her wet cheek, and then climbing into the big carriage.

Gazella beamed with happiness, and hugged Willow so hard that her little brown eyes seemed to grow larger. But her tail was still whipping, so Longarm knew the dog was happy.

Come to think of it, so was he when he managed not to think of his friend Wade and this long-planned but ill-fated fishing vacation.

Watch for

LONGARM AND THE SHEEP WAR

249th novel in the exciting LONGARM series
from Jove

Coming in September!

Explore the exciting Old West with one of the men who made it wild!

Prices slightly higher in Canada